I HEART
BEAT

Move over Jacqueline Wilson – Edyth Bulbring is the new queen of fiction.
The Weekender for I HEART BEAT

The hectic pace of the dramas and April-May's own largely benign view of them make this is a fresh and entertaining novel which reveals that teen trouble is the same the whole world over.
Lovereading4kids for A MONTH WITH APRIL-MAY

I devoured the book in one sitting, but it passed the acid test when my teenage daughter was compelled by the sheer excellence of the writing to keep reading.

The Times South Africa for A MONTH WITH APRIL-MAY

I HEART BEAT

EDYTH BULBRING

HOT
KEY
BOOKS

First published in Great Britain in 2014 by Hot Key Books
Northburgh House, 10 Northburgh Street, London EC1V 0AT
First published as The Summer of Toffie and Grummer by Oxford University Press Southern
Africa in 2008

Copyright © Edyth Bulbring 2007

A CIP catalogue record for this book is available from the British Library.

ISBN: 978-1-4714-0061-2

1

This book is typeset in 11pt Sabon using Atomik ePublisher
Printed and bound by Clays Ltd, St Ives Plc

FSC

Hot Key Books supports the Forest Stewardship Council (FSC),
the leading international forest certification organisation, and is committed to printing only on
Greenpeace-approved FSC-certified paper.

www.hotkeybooks.com

Hot Key Books is part of the Bonnier Publishing Group
www.bonnierpublishing.com

For Sophie

Part One

Chapter 1

I SPEND THE first morning of my Christmas holidays scraping vomit off my bedroom carpet. I use an egg lifter, which makes it easier to get at the bits of pineapple and mushroom. Mom appears at the door. Every one of her thirty-five years hangs in the saggy bags under her bloodshot eyes.

"Aw, dolling. What can I say? There was something wrong with the pizza. I just couldn't keep it down," she says, looking at the red stains on the carpet.

There was nothing wrong with the pizza. It must've been the bottle of vodka that she downed to help it on its way. I tell her she's a pathetic mess and wave her out of my room. I'll bring her some tea and fried eggs when I'm done.

"You're a doll," Mom says and stumbles out.

I'm not a doll at all. Just used to it all. It doesn't help getting too uptight.

All my friends — well the only two that I have — complain about their parents a lot. The mothers are always on their cases about their messy rooms, their school marks, etcetera, etcetera. Just boring and ugly.

And the fathers. Well, that's another story. My friends find them totally embarrassing. They're loud and make stupid remarks. Just plain gross.

I think they're okay to have just two gross, stupid fathers between them. I've had five on my own and I'm only fourteen years old. My real dad ducked two hours after I was born. I could trip over him in the street and I wouldn't recognise him. Since then, there's been Paul, Winston, Guido, and the last one was Wally. And he was a complete one!

He left last week. Correction: Mom chucked

him out, like she did all the others. I wonder who cheated on who. I don't think it was Mom this time. Oh well, what goes around comes around.

She's been behaving like a complete nutcase since Wally left. Off work for six days and drinking like a thirsty whale. It's back to rehab for Mom. I don't know why she doesn't buy shares in that clinic. She's their most loyal customer. Correction: Mom is the Dunkeld West Drankwinkel's best customer.

When she goes into the bottle store, Mr Khumalo always says, "You're my best customer, Mrs Double-Yoo."

And Ms Wellbeloved — that's Mom — goes, "And you're my favourite shop manager, Mr Kay." And they laugh together like old alkies.

I take Mom some breakfast and find her on the phone. It must be Grummer. Mom always gets that face when she's talking to her mother: all cringing and defiant.

"Don't be like that, Moo. I can't help it. It's in the genes," she says. "Blame your father for my disease ... Yes, it *is* a disease, Moo, and you've got to respect that. Stop moaning at me like I actually have a choice in this."

The phone is under her chin and she's plucking her eyebrows as she talks. That's also in the genes, courtesy of Grummer and her crowd; we're a very hairy family. If Mom doesn't deal with her brows on a weekly basis she gets a uni-brow, like a long hairy caterpillar above her eyes. Argggh!

My legs are so hairy they're like permanent yeti boots all the way up to my knees. Mom says she'll take me for a wax when she can get it together. Until then, I wear pants, even in summer. I hate hair: it's so untidy.

Mom dabs some spit on her puffy brow and says to Grummer, "I'm checking in to that place tomorrow and I'll be there for four weeks … What do you mean it's such short notice and you hardly know her? She's your grandchild for heavensakes. You get to spend some quality time with her."

Mom stabs the duvet with her tweezers as she makes her points. "I'll put her on the plane from Johannesburg tomorrow and you can meet her in Cape Town. The two of you can spend a lovely holiday together and I'll be out of rehab by the time she comes back."

Mom's forehead stays unwrinkled as she listens to Grummer on the other side of the phone. But I know she's getting mad. That's the good thing with Botox: most people can't tell when you're annoyed. Mom gets her injections every three months. Her brow is as smooth as a baby's bum.

"Nothing's really changed, Moo, so stop panicking. It's just that I won't be spending the holiday with you. Get on with the garden like you planned ... Jesus, Moo, it's not like I've ever asked you for much. For once in your life help me out here ... Sorry, I didn't mean to take your Lord's name in vain ... Gimme a break man, Moo ..." And she rolls her eyes at me.

There's a long silence as Mom and Grummer chew on their anger. I leave the room and go and make some green tea. When I go back to Mom's room, she's finished talking to Grummer and is tucking in to the greasy eggs. There's yolk on her chin. Sis! She's beyond disgusting.

"It's all settled: Moo and you will spend the

holidays together without me. I know it's not ideal and all, but I can't help it."

Talk about an understatement! I hardly know my grandmother. In fact, I've seen her like seven times in my life and half of those were when I was a baby. Then Mom and Grummer fell out and there haven't been any visits for five years.

Trust Mom to mess it all up. The plan had been to go to Mom's new holiday house in some trendy dorp near Cape Town for four weeks. The house is one of Mom's investments. For a complete loser she's rolling in cash. She owns an advertising agency.

It's useful that she's the boss and has a hot-shot Number Two to do all the work 'cos she takes so much time off being a drunk. She sometimes says, "God, I'm going to get fired! No, I'm not, I'm the boss." And then she laughs like a complete idiot. She can be so not funny.

I dunno why she invited Grummer along on holiday. Maybe it's 'cos Grandpa died six months ago and Mom's feeling bad about being such a lousy daughter. I suppose if I didn't make it to my dad's funeral I would also feel like a cow. Well, maybe not.

"I know you don't like gardening," Mom says to me while lighting a cigarette, "but Moo will be busy with that. I'm sure you'll find something else to do."

Yeah, like what? I pass her the ashtray. Mom ignores my hand and flicks ash into her eggs. How, I ask myself for the millionth time, how could I be related to this woman?

"Hell, Bea, don't look at me like that. Fix Moo up with another husband. Pull her a new man. Get her off my back. Find her someone just like your boring grandpa who'll keep her away from us for the next twenty years. Make it a project." She stubs her ciggie out into my teacup.

Hiss!

Chapter 2

I'VE GOT A zillion things to do today. Before I went to bed last night I made a "To Do" list on my cellphone. I make lists a lot. If I don't, my tummy feels like it's talking Chinese.

My "To Do" list looks like this:

1. Book flight to Cape Town
2. Inform Grummer about flight arrangements
3. Book taxis for Mom and me
4. Shop for holiday necessities
5. Pack for Mom and me

6. Empty fridge and put out garbage
7. Lock up and put on security alarm

Mom's still sleeping. She cleaned out the booze in the house last night (one of the rehab rules) and ended up drinking a lot of it.

"Such a terrible, shocking, miserable waste to pour it all down the drain," she protested when I got up to lock the doors and turn off the lights around about midnight. I left her talking to the toilet seat and went back to bed.

It's now 6:00 a.m. GMT. The clock by Mom's bed says eight o'clock. She and the rest of the country live in South African time, which is two hours ahead of Greenwich Mean Time now it's summer. What losers!

I ignore Mom's wet snores and action my "To Do" list after a breakfast of green tea and eight wedges of grapefruit.

I get my laptop, go online and book my ticket to Cape Town using Mom's credit card. I text Grummer the flight number and arrival time. I send my school photo to her cellphone so she can recognise me. I book a taxi for three hours before my flight. We can do Mom first and then I can go off to the airport. I smother my face in sunscreen, put on my shades (black) and walk the three blocks to the mall. I hate shopping, but I have a whole list of things I need to get. My shopping list looks like this:

1. green tea (with fruit infusion)
2. sunscreen (factor 50$^+$)
3. sun hat (black)
4. hairbands (black)
5. pants (black)
6. memory stick for laptop (black)

The shop assistant at the clothing store won't leave me alone in the changing room. I've taken seven pairs of pants and nothing will fit. I can't bear the lights and the mirrors. I close my eyes while I take off the pants and look away while I pull on the next pair.

"We have a forty per cent discount on teenage bras," the old bag says, sticking her face around the curtain. She looks at my chest like a housewife assessing fresh bread.

I want to impale myself on the clothes hanger. I don't wear a bra; I never want to get breasts. If I ever grow a pair like Mom's I'll kill myself. I hate breasts. They're so untidy.

I buy three pairs of pants on Mom's account and finish up the rest of the shop at the supermarket.

Mom's shuffling around in the kitchen when I get home. "I hate myself. I hate my life. I'm such a useless mother. You must hate me. You'd be better off without a mother like me," she says, spreading butter onto burnt toast.

Affirmative. I say nothing and clean up the kitchen and dump all the food from the fridge into the bin. While Mom showers, I complete my "To Do" list.

The taxi's hooting outside and I put on all the downstairs lights and turn on the alarm.

"We can text each other all the time. They give you your cellphone back after one week. And I'll be online then too, so email me everything that's happening. It'll be like we're pen pals," Mom says.

Yeah, like really, what *is* this woman smoking?

In the taxi, Mom holds my hand tightly. My palm starts to sweat. I try to take my hand away, but she holds on.

"I promise this is the last time. It won't happen again. I swear to you, things will be different in four weeks," Mom says.

The situation's becoming so totally embarrassing. I wish Mom would learn some new lines.

Mom and me give each other awkward hugs outside the gates of Promises Rehab Clinic.

"You're my girl. You'll always be my girl," Mom says, looking all crazy.

Yeah, whatever. I tell her I can't book her in — I have a plane to catch. I leave her chatting up the security guard.

On the plane, I sit next to another kid, who picks his nose all the way to Cape Town. Really digs in there. It's a totally awesome performance.

The air hostess gives him this really lame entertainment pack and asks what we want to drink.

"Virgin Mary," I say. She looks at me weirdly.

I spell it out for her: tomato juice, no vodka, no ice. Tabasco and salt and pepper and a slice of lemon on the side. What kind of training do these people have? She finally gets it.

I give the "chicken or beef?" a miss. The kid next to me takes a break from his nasal excavation and tucks in to the beef. He picks out the pieces of meat with his fingers, avoiding the peas. I try to forget that I saw where he'd recently put his fingers. Eeeeuuuuw!

I arrive to the sound of my name being broadcast across the arrivals hall: "Could Beatrice Wellbeloved please come to the information counter in arrivals. Her grandmother is waiting for her." This is repeated about a million times until I think I'm in one of those freaky time loops from a science fiction movie. After collecting my luggage, I sprint over to the information counter.

"Grummer?" I say.

The woman standing in front of me has a pink circle on each of her cheeks and looks like she's having a hernia.

"Beatrice! Beatrice! Thank God I've found you." And she really looks like she's thanking God 'cos she's rubbing a gold cross around her neck.

Grummer's been waiting for me for five hours. She couldn't get hold of Mom and never got my text message and photo on her cellphone. She tells me she doesn't know what a text message is. I'm dealing with a complete techno retard here.

We get into her car — a real dinosaur from the dark seventies — and for the next hour Grummer tells me again and again about how she waited and waited for me at the airport and how she waited and waited.

The next four weeks with Grummer are going to be very long.

Roll on holiday from hell!

Chapter 3

AS SOON AS we get into the car to leave the airport (although whether you could call this 1975 Ford Cortina a car is debatable), I hit the MapInfo website on my cellphone and get the directions to our destination. My cellphone is my most valuable accessory. Mom got it off a client, and I took it off Mom. It can do practically anything — anything except eat or drink.

Grummer isn't keen on newfangled technology (yes, "newfangled" is still a word in current use by her generation). She has a mapbook, and every few kilometres she pulls over and checks that she's following the correct route. When she's not reading the mapbook, she drives like a snail on tranquilizers.

I think it's when we make the third wrong turn in twenty minutes that I decide to do what Mom suggested in her babalaas state yesterday morning: I'll fix Grummer up with a new husband just like Grandpa. I'll pull her a nice old wrinklie and they can be happy together — far, far away from me. Being forced into another holiday with Grummer will turn me into a head case.

I decide on a name for my matchmaking project: Pulling for Grummer. I use the nightmare journey for a bit of research. I'm going to need to know what I'll be dealing with, so I do an intensive client survey.

It's not hard to get Grummer to talk about herself. She tells me about the retirement village where she has a little house in Port Elizabeth, a small coastal town a day's drive from Cape Town where the wind doesn't stop blowing. Except she calls this windy hell-hole Pee-Eee. Just when I'm getting really excited (not) about the goings-on at

18

this happening place, Grummer starts up about her love for Jesus: how she likes to go to church and talk to God; how much strength God gives her to get through difficulties; how God talks to her when she's clipping her toenails … On and on. Okay, Grummer, too much detail.

Next, she's full-steam ahead about her sewing group. Yes, I love patchwork quilts too, Grummer (not). Oh, and the garden. Sigh! (The sigh is Grummer's. Mine's the mute yawn that gives my face a stitch.)

After two hours Grummer isn't talking any more — even *she* finds herself boring — and I'm done with my list of questions. I take a photo of her with my cellphone (in profile, not her best) and enter a brief text snapshot. I'll fill in the detail later. As it stands, the client snapshot looks like this:

THE CLIENT
Name: Mavis Wellbeloved
Age: Sixty
Physical characteristics: height: one metre

sixty-five, green eyes, bushy brown hair cut into neat cap, rounded body with orange-peel upper arms, prickly legs (a bad home-job)

Dress style: Low budget clothing stores like Aye Cee Kermans (losers call it Ackermans), Pep, Mr Price (no style)

Hobbies: church, sewing, gardening, reading (historical romances), classical music, walking

Marital status: recently widowed with one useless daughter and one granddaughter

Dietary requirements: a balanced diet, everything in moderation, absolutely no alcohol

Media preferences: television (the news, weather and some soaps), radio (the news, weather and classical music)

Sleep patterns: early to bed; early to rise (at least eight hours' sleep)

That's it. Let's face it: I don't have a lot to work with here.

I fiddle with Grummer's cellphone. It's one of those that came in when cellphones were first invented, like a hundred years ago. I listen to the voice message. It goes like this: "Hello, this is Derek Wellbeloved. Mavis and I aren't able to come to the telephone right now, but please leave a message and one of us will return your telephone call as soon as we are able ... how do you stop this thing? Mavis, which button must I press?" And then there's lots of shuffling and the message ends.

Well, that's no good now, is it? We can't have a prospective squeeze for Grummer calling her and getting this message. He'll think she's already got someone.

"Grummer," I say. "Grummer, you've got a very old message on your cellphone. Why don't you change it?"

"I don't know how to," she says. Grummer's knuckles are white on the steering wheel.

"No problem, I'll just quickly do it for you." I start to push a couple of buttons.

"No, don't. Leave my telephone alone. It's not a

toy." Grummer sounds all shrill. She gets the pink circles on her cheeks. Then she says in a calmer voice, "I like to telephone myself sometimes and listen to that message ... when I want to hear your grandfather's voice."

Ka-ching! I hear the sound of The Jackpot. I quickly text my two and only friends back home, go online and upload Grummer's comment to our corny comment blog. Within minutes they text me their response. It's rated a big ten. Top score. They're going to struggle to beat it. Yee-ha!

I say nothing to Grummer. One doesn't want to encourage too much sharing. But I take stock of Project: Pulling for Grummer. She's not great material to start with, and now I hear that she's still got a thing for the dead guy. Things aren't looking up. I'll have to charge double my normal rate. Ha-ha!

We finally come to the turn-off for the village and it's pretty dark. We've been on the road for four hours. Not too bad for a two-hour journey. Way to go, Grummer! I make a quick mental note: do not enter Grummer as a contestant in

The Amazing Race. She would be the one still dithering about at the starting line while all the other participants had already made it home.

Our dream holiday home for the next four weeks (twenty-seven days and three hours) is set far back on a piece of jungle. We make it up the driveway, and Grummer manages to park without completely taking out a guava tree.

We find the front door using my cellphone as a torch. As I unlock the door I hear the sound of the ocean. Now isn't that nice, hey? We're twenty kilometres from the beach and still it's like the sea is on our doorstep.

As I turn off the alarm I feel water soak into my takkies. My feet are soon wet through.

Grummer finds the light switch and we look around us; we're standing in a pond. There are a million cockroaches floating tummy-side up as well as a couple of bloated cats. Correction: they're rats. Well, that makes me feel so much better (not).

I follow the sound of the waterfall to the bathroom. It's the geyser, gushing water all over the place. It's been doing this for a long time 'cos the house is swamped.

Typical! Well done, Georgia Wellbeloved, you've done it again. Trust Mom to buy a house and leave it unattended for nine months. Grummer says it: "How could Georgia do this to me? It's so typical of your mother. Can she never do anything right?"

Hold it right there, Grummer! That's my mother you're badmouthing. No one gets to trash Mom but me. It's *my* perk. I'll have to set her straight on this later.

"I think we may need to telephone a plumber," Grummer says.

Yeah, like duh!

Chapter 4

I STAND OUTSIDE on the grass and text "plumber" to Info Service. In a few minutes three names and numbers land in my inbox. The first is Appel, the second is Dreyer and the third is Pretorius. I like to do things methodically, so I call the first.

A voice answers and shouts over the sound of loud music: "Just hold on. I've got to take this outside. I can't hear a blerrie thing in here. Hey man, Pine, just keep an eye on my beer while I get this, hey."

And then I hear a male voice jeering: "So the

wife's finally got you. It's home James for you."
And then there's a lot of laughter.

Grummer's sweeping water out of the front door. It's pouring out onto the veranda.

I brief Mr Appel on the problem. "Jislaaik," he exclaims in dismay. "That's not good. All that water. And there's a drought on and water restrictions. Your water bill's going to be a killer."

I don't care about a drought or water restrictions. I just want the water to stop pouring out of the geyser.

Mr Appel says he'll be here in two ticks. He's in the pubbingrill on the main road.

It's two ticks and forty minutes later and Mr Appel arrives in a bakkie. The side of the vehicle says: An Appel a day keeps your plumbing OK. There's someone with him. An alarm goes off in my head as a fat kid walks towards me. Loser Alert! He's wearing khaki shorts, slip-slops and a T-shirt with a collar. I try to snap a photo of him with my cellphone, but he won't keep still. Damn, my two and only friends back home will never believe me.

"Sorry hey, I had a couple more dops for the road," Mr Appel says to Grummer. His breath smells to me like he's had more than just a couple.

"But I'm here now, so let's fix the problem," he says.

Grummer takes him through to the bathroom, and me and Loser get to spend some special time together. I don't think it gets any sweeter than this: Loser's name is Christoffel, but I must call him Toffie. Yip! Toffie Appel, get it?

But it gets better. His uncle the plumber's name is Art. He's not joking — Art Appel. Am I the only one in the world who thinks calling someone Potato in Afrikaans is freaksville? And just when I thought I had died and gone to loser heaven, he hands me the olive in the cocktail: his dad, the guy who owns the pubbingrill in the main road, is Pine. I don't think I need to spell it out. Are these people for real?

There's no time for any more relatives 'cos Mr Potato, the boozy plumber, is done. He's managed to turn off the water for now and he'll be back tomorrow to turn it back on and finish the job.

I can't wait. If he doesn't bring his nephew and brother along with him, I'll be a wreck; a family portrait for the loser gallery blog will mean a big score for me.

I'm feeling hungry so I call Info for Mr Delivery to get some take-outs. Mr Who? They don't have him registered in the area database. I've landed in the middle of the dark ages. Things can't get worse. Then they do.

Grummer's getting some stuff out of a plastic packet. She calls it supper. "I thought we would be peckish when we arrived, so I brought along one or two things to tide us over until we can shop tomorrow," she says, opening some Tupperware containers.

I pick the raisins out of the rusks and take some pieces of cucumber from the salad. There's creamy dressing on the cucumber so I pass and stick to the raisins. Grummer eats carefully with a plastic knife and fork and uses a tissue to dab her lips. I like a neat eater. I make a mental note to add this quality to her client snapshot.

"If your grandfather had been here, things

would have been hunky-dory," Grummer says. "You know he was a dentist? He could always fix fiddly things. He was so good with his hands. He always carried a toolbox with him for 'in case'."

In between careful mouthfuls, Grummer talks about the dead guy. As she rambles on, she starts to dab her eyes with the tissue. Oh no, Grummer, don't you dare! I'm not big on crying. I can't cry. A bit like Nelson Mandela, except I didn't mess up my tear ducts in a quarry. My tears just dried up five years back when Guido left. Correction: when Mom chucked him out and then went on to Husband Number Five.

Before Grummer gets out of hand, I check out the house. It's full of the previous owner's stuff, even their old towels and sheets. Eeeeuuuuw!

Mom bought it like this to save all the hassle of doing it herself. That's my Mom: a one hundred per cent proof slob.

I take the bedroom off the lounge, and Grummer chooses the one off the kitchen. I think there's enough space between us. My bedroom's damp. I strip the bed and put a bath towel on the pillow.

I find a sheet that was white in a former life.

I lie on the bed and count all the bamboo sticks on the ceiling. There are 387 bamboo sticks. I get up and count all the stone tiles on the floor — 172. After that, my tummy finally stops shouting.

Before I go to brush and floss, I do some essential preparation for tomorrow. I upload the text snapshot and photo of Grummer from my cellphone to my laptop and open a special file called Project: Pulling for Grummer. I then make a few brief notes on snapshot number two. The target snapshot looks like this:

THE TARGET

Name: Lucky Mr X

Age: between fifty-five and sixty-three (Grandpa was sixty-four, but I need to go younger so he can outlast Grummer)

Employment: in the professions (dentist preferably, like Grandpa, but could also be a doctor, lawyer, engineer, architect, etcetera)

Religion: nutter like Grummer and

Grandpa

Social habits: teetotaller (like Grummer and Grandpa), neat and well mannered — especially at the table

Physical characteristics: appropriate bodily hair (none on back), good teeth (preferably target's own), a Grandpa clone

Marital status: single. Widow or bachelor (must not be divorced)

Dietary requirements: absolutely no alcohol

Hobbies: see text snapshot of Grummer

Media preferences: see text snapshot of Grummer

Sleep patterns: see text snapshot of Grummer

I realise I'm not quite cracking it and save the file to my new memory stick. I get my cellphone and make a quick "To Do" list for tomorrow. It looks like this:

1. Shop for essentials: mite spray, cockroach spray, rat poison
2. Clean house
3. Buy more airtime off Mom's credit card for cellphone (running low)
4. Research professional geriatrics living in the dorp
5. Make a list of venues where geriatrics hang out

I do my bathroom routine (no water until Mr Potato fixes it tomorrow, argggh!), take the bands out of my hair and put a stocking on my head to keep the hair out of my face. I rub cream on my feet and put on a pair of socks. It's now 10:00 p.m. GMT. Midnight for losers. There are twenty-seven days left to accomplish Project: Pulling for Grummer.

I add a last point to my "To Do" list:
FOCUS!

Chapter 5

I SPEND THE first three minutes after waking up counting the mosquito bites on my body. The overnight feeding frenzy has left me with twenty-eight bites. I add "buy mosquito net" to my "To Do" list.

Grummer's up before me. Long before. She's had her morning walk and picked up a few things from the café. The radio's playing classical music (boring).

"I think a person's routine is so important," says Grummer as she straightens the knives and forks on the breakfast table. "I always like to take my little walk before breakfast. It helps me decide on all the things I need to do in the day."

Oh great, a closet list-maker.

Grummer cuts grapefruit into eight wedges and arranges them carefully on the plates. There's a pot of rooibos tea for her and green tea (with fruit infusion) for me. Clever Grummer to buy bottled water while we weather the drought until Mr Potato returns. The toast is keeping warm under a tea cosy.

Before Grummer sits down she listens to the nine o'clock news. She stands for the full broadcast, then she sighs and turns off the radio. "Now we can eat breakfast. I always like to do things properly, don't you?"

Sure do, Grummer.

Grummer's "To Do" list is impressive. She ticks the items off with her fingers in between bites of marmalade toast: clean house, get geyser fixed, shop to stock the fridge, assess garden ...

I could pick up some tips from Grummer. She includes personal tasks like finishing her novel, listening to the afternoon classical music programme on the radio and watching her soapie *7de Laan*. Freaky!

I finish my grapefruit and eat some toast. Then I eat a tablespoon of marmalade. (I like to keep my foods separate.) Grummer gives me the kind of look I keep in reserve for weird people. She offers to make me some marmalade toast. "There's nothing like hot, buttery marmalade toast," she says. I tell her there's nothing doing.

After breakfast I go outside to assess the jungle. I take some photos with my cellphone from different angles. This is what they look like: one photo shows seven guava trees running across the lawn. They are six point four metres from the veranda. They are so big they hide the view of the mountain. Another photo is of a lawn of green jellyfish. Correction: they're weeds. The third has three rickety shacks in the middle of the lawn. The last is of a forest of scrawny trees at the bottom of the garden. My assessment of the garden: Grummer's going to be very busy. Too busy to bug me. I'm satisfied.

A bakkie pulls up and Mr Potato gets out. He's

alone. He goes and does his thing to the geyser and chats to Grummer. He gives her names of people who can help with the garden and the name of a cleaning service. I hope they're relatives.

"Old Toffie says I must say his hullos to you, " Mr Potato tells me. "He's helping at the bar this morning, but he says he'll pull in later. He liked you a lot, hey?" And then he winks.

Is this creature talking to *me*?

Grummer looks pleased. "I think it will be lovely for Beatrice to have a young friend in the village. Don't you think so, Beatrice?"

Sure, Grummer. I put a finger in the middle of my tongue and make a cotching noise (in my head).

While Grummer makes like a million phone calls, I check out the local phone directory for some professionals (point four on my "To Do" list). There are two doctors, a construction company and an attorney's office. I capture their numbers on my cellphone.

I call the doctors first. The one is dead (not a good recommendation) and the other is away for two weeks. I draw a blank with the construction company. They don't have engineers or architects. Just builders. The attorney has moved twenty kilometres away to Hermanus by the sea, where business is booming. The list of professional targets is a sum of one: the absent GP. Dr Peter Waterford. A clean-sounding name that.

I action point five on my "To Do" list ("check out geriatric hangouts") and compile a list of Target Venues. Everybody knows old people need to do a lot of sucking up to God in the short time they have left before they kick the bucket, so I start with the churches. There are four of them: Anglican, Dutch Reformed, Methodist and Catholic. Sundays must be one big party in this dorp.

Old people are always sick, so I include Dr Peter Waterford's surgery on my list of Target Venues.

While I'm filling in the detail, the fairies arrive. There's nothing magical about them. There's one big Afrikaans lady and four uniformed middle-aged helpers, armed with cleaning equipment.

The big lady introduces herself to Grummer.

Her name is Davonne Huiseman and she runs Fairies Unlimited, the village's house-cleaning service. She doesn't bother introducing her girls (she calls them this), but they bob and grimace at Grummer.

Grummer asks them their names and introduces herself. She tells them they are fine young women and they are a lifesaver. (Her eyes go all squiffy at Mrs Huiseman when she says the women word.)

Grummer then leaves them to the filthy house and takes off for the shops in Hermanus — to get out of their way. I slap on some sunscreen (factor 50+), a hat (black), shades (black) and hit the big city on foot to scope the Target Venues.

The dorp has one main street and it's laid out on a nice neat grid. I walk the grid methodically. In the middle is a large village green and there's a church on each of the four corners. I check out the noticeboards and make a note of the services. I ignore all the other bumf on Mother's Union meetings, the Wednesday night Bible study groups and the choir practices (don't want to get too carried away now, do I?).

Dr Peter Waterford's surgery is in the main street next to the Spar. His receptionist (Marlene) says he's in Jozi (she pronounces the city where I live "Joh-Hunnersburg") and will be back in two weeks. Lucky Dr Waterford.

There's not a lot more to see. The hairdresser's next to the library. Her window says she is Sunette, recently of London. She's not in. The temp says she's gone to Cape Town to have her veins stripped. All the standing she does has made her legs look like a 3D road-map. Shame.

On the side of the main road is a set of fake traffic lights. They stand at the entrance to a building. The lights show green, which tells customers it's open. I'm looking at the dorp's drinking hole: the pubbingrill, or as the sign says: Pub & Grill. The blackboard outside offers the best steaks in the province and a spit braai on Sundays. Can't wait. Barbecueing dead animals on a big stick are so my thing (not).

"Hey, you came to find me. That's nice, hey? I'm nearly finished here taking out the empties."

The loser is squinting at me on the pavement.

I give him a good, long look through my shades. This is what I see: one, short, fat, kid.

His face is a galaxy of freckles (needs factor 50$^+$ fast). He's got big brown cow eyes with lots of lash accessory (what a waste). He's wearing a horizontal-striped T-shirt which makes his tummy look like a contour map and it's tucked into — dare I say it — blue polyester shorts.

He looks at me back. "Shame, you must be so hot. Give me ten minutes and then we can go to your place and you can change into your cossie. I know the best place to swim by the river."

Fat chance, fat boy!

Chapter 6

TOFFIE DOESN'T DO rejection well. He follows me home on his bike and then churns it down the road, ringing his bell through the stop signs so he gets there first. He's sweating by the gate.

"I'm the winner," he says like it was some kind of race.

The fairies have flown away and Grummer's packing away the groceries.

"Jis, your house is smart, hey?" Toffie says. His eyes are big with awe.

I watch him looking around the open-plan lounge, dining room and kitchen.

I get a horrible shock: Toffie's a Counter. I recognise the signs. His eyes zoom in on the bamboo-covered ceilings. Click. Click. Click. There are 1,292 sticks of bamboo on the ceilings. I do the calculations with him.

Before I know it, his eyes are on the terracotta-tiled floors. Click. Click. Click. There are 452 tiles.

That's enough, Toffie. This is *my* house. *My* scores. I don't share my habits with losers.

Grummer packs me some fruit and bottled water in a bag, and I grab sunscreen (factor 50⁺), shades (black) and a towel (black).

I make sure my cellphone battery is fully charged. I see some brilliant opportunities for visual material coming up. Prepare yourself for stardom, Toffie!

"You can ride the bike and I'll walk if you like," Toffie offers. Charmed, I'm sure. Grummer has one better: "There are two bicycles in the garage. They came with the house," she says.

I don't do bikes.

Toffie takes me to this place by the river. To get

there, we have to walk through someone's front yard. He says it's quite legal. No one's allowed to own the river. The lady of the house looks seriously peed off. I give her one of my special merry waves.

Toffie eats the fruit and I drink bottled water and watch him eat. He cuts the oranges into quarters with his penknife and, after sucking all the flesh, carves orange-peel teeth. What a scream (not).

He eats a couple of pears one after the other with pips and skins. Sis! He likes to get as much of his face as possible covered in juice. He puts me right off my water.

"What, aren't you eating? Are you on a diet, hey?"

Oh, pahleez!

He says he's on a diet. It's called the Seafood Diet. "I see food and I eat it," he says. He laughs like a blocked drain. Oh great, I'm trapped at the river with the village idiot.

It's hot and I smear on sunscreen (factor 50+). Toffie laughs when I offer him some. "That's for girls," he says.

He strips down to his jocks. Correction: it's a Speedo. The ultimate fashion statement.

He takes a flying leap off the jetty and does a huge belly flop. My cellphone records this in full-colour video with sound. He doesn't let up for fifteen minutes. He forward-flops and back-flips and flops and flips. Then he throws himself onto his towel.

"So come on, get in. The water's lekker, man," he says and starts to pick fluff out of his belly button.

I shake my head. As nice as the water is, I don't think so.

He looks at me all mournfully. "Ag, sorry man. That time of the month, hey? You've got the ladies' problem."

I have not! I've never had a period. End of discussion.

"Do you have terrible cramps? My sister gets them so bad she can't walk. She calls her time of the month 'Monica', but in her diary she spells it like 'Moniker'. What name do you call yours?"

I call it my business.

His sister — her name is Adore. (Adore Appel —
get it? I nearly wet myself.) Well, Adore works in
the video shop. It operates out of the garage at
the entrance to the dorp. One of the highlights I
missed on my recce of the village this morning.

Talking of video shops reminds me, it's home-
movie time. I show Toffie his fifteen minutes of
glory. I've got some great close-ups of the tummy.
And then his face when the snot poured out of
his nose after he sucked water up the wrong way.

"Ag, jis, just look at that cool dive. Play that
again. And that one — you see how I twist there?"

I pause on the tummy shot to make a point.

Toffie laughs hard. "Ag, no man, Beat. Don't
look at my rolls. Ma says it's just puppy fat."

Beat? Like, who's Beat? I'll Beat his head in.

Toffie says he's mad for the movie. He wishes he
could put it on a videotape to give to his parents
for Christmas.

I tell him I'll send it to his cellphone. He says
he doesn't have one. I nearly pass out from shock.
I tell him I'll email him instructions on how his

sister can upload it off a website from her video shop computer and burn it onto DVD. Poor Toffie looks at me like I'm from outer space.

He leans over my shoulder while I get it sorted. While emailing to Toffie's brand new email address that I created for him — *fatloser@gmail.com* — he leans in even closer.

"Hey, Beat, you've got hair on the top of your lip. It looks soft like a baby duck," he says, lifting his finger like he's going to stroke my hairy face.

I get to my feet. It really is enough already.

We pass the pubbingrill on the way home. I'm used to bars. In fact, if I ever had to go on a quiz show and there was a "name the bar in Johannesburg where you can get a drink any time in the morning" question, I could name eight. I go to a good school for that kind of thing. Ha-ha.

There's a lady behind the bar smoking a cigarette. Toffie introduces me to his mom who, in between puffs, is putting clean glasses away with the forty-three others on the shelf (three chipped).

"Hey, Ma, there are two glasses missing," Toffie

46

says, blinking at the shelf.

Blast! This kid's real trouble. Losers aren't supposed to be Counters.

"You must come tomorrow for the spit braai," Mrs Appel says. "Everyone in the dorp comes — and you look like you could do with some meat on your bones."

I don't do meat — or barbecues — or people.

Mrs Appel's name is Brenda. I try every combo I can think of to make her name fit in with the rest of her corny family. But nothing works. Hmph!

I leave the bar and go back to the house.

Grummer's sitting outside on the veranda reading her book. She marks her page with a tasselled book marker and tells me it's lunch time. We're having salad and quiche.

I eat the lettuce first and then the baby tomatoes. I pick the mushrooms out of the egg goo and leave the crust of the quiche.

Grummer likes to mix and match her food. A bit of quiche and salad with a dab of dressing balances on her fork. She leaves her plate spotless.

"Your new friend Christoffel has such a

pleasant, open face. I liked him immediately," she says, clearing the plates.

Red Alert! Grummer's been had. I know Toffie's a freak. He acts like a loser but he's got dark, sneaky counting habits. I'm going to have to look out for Grummer if she acts this trusting around everybody.

There's a knock on the door. It's delivered by a big, hairy hand.

Argggh!

Chapter 7

THE BIG HAIRY hand belongs to Mr du Plooy. He's the man who's going to help Grummer get the garden into shape. I make a mental note to google this character. The chances are we're related. He does hair in a big way. It sticks out of the top of his long socks. It glares at me in bristling tufts through the buttonholes of his khaki shirt and climbs all the way to the top of his neck. Can't wait to see his back.

I follow at a careful distance while Grummer tells him what she wants. She ticks off the items with her fingers. The guava trees have to go, all seven of them. What's the point of having a home with a mountain view (as the property advertisement claimed) when all you'll be able to see every winter are rotting guavas?

Mr du Plooy frowns. All of them? He's not pleased. There's nothing like the taste of a ripe guava or fifty in the winter. Grummer says yes. Mr du Plooy says no. Grummer looks uncertain.

She wants some oak and elm trees at the bottom of the garden. Most of the existing trees must come out. Mr du Plooy concurs. Yes, the rooikrans trees must go; they're invaders. But the quince trees must stay.

Grummer says no. She wants all the old quince trees gone. Mr du Plooy frowns. All they need is a bit of spraying and pruning. There's nothing quite like quince jam in the autumn. Grummer puts her foot in a vrot quince and flounders. She winces as her shoe sinks into the rotten fruit.

There's a lot more to be done. Grummer wants a pond at the centre of the garden with beds of roses. Mr du Plooy raises the question of water. Ponds and roses need lots of it. Planting indigenous is the way to go in a place where summer rain is scarce. Grummer is firm; she wants a rose garden, not indigenous fynbos.

Mr du Plooy shrugs and suggests an irrigation system. The house is entitled to leiwater twice a week. All the houses in the old part of the village get the overflow of water from the spring which is channelled in ditches along the sides of the roads.

Grummer says she'll look at the finances.

Then there's the herb garden around the back at the kitchen door. They agree. Grummer sighs with relief. They reach deadlock over a veggie garden. Grummer says she doesn't want vegetables in her garden. Her late husband always said they looked untidy.

Mr du Plooy says there's nothing untidy about a fine cabbage and a head of lettuce. Grummer and Mr du Plooy sulk.

Lastly, the falling-down garden shacks must get knocked down. Mr du Plooy gets a bit edgy. The two spitting porcupines that are nesting at the top of his eyes meet together in attack formation.

"They're not garden shacks, Mrs Wellbeloved,"

he says. "With all due respect, these were people's homes."

I look at the old shacks. Homes — schmomes!

Mr du Plooy tells Grummer a long (boring) story about how a coloured family used to live on the land where Mom's holiday house is now standing. They grew fruit and vegetables on the plot until they were forced to move in the sixties because of apartheid. They were among numerous coloured families who were moved off their plots along the river by the government to make way for white people

Grummer looks uncomfortable. "Oh dear, that wasn't right, was it?" she says and Mr du Plooy shakes his head.

I get cross. There are a couple of things Mr du Plooy doesn't quite get. The first is that Grummer is the client. The second is that the client is never wrong. The third is that even when the client is wrong, the service provider doesn't tell the client. I know these three golden rules from Mom.

Before I can set Mr du Plooy straight on these principles, Grummer offers him some tea. He takes coffee (black) with three sugars (white).

While they sit outside on the veranda and discuss things, I check out Grummer's bedroom. On the bedside table next to the *Good News Bible* is a photo of the dead guy holding a cat.

I come away with a list of the following characteristics: he's tall — maybe one metre eighty-two, but it's difficult to tell 'cos he's sitting down. He's adequately haired. He's on the bony side and his mouth has the look of a turtle. Thin and stern. He's a cat lover. His eyes (the dead guy's, not the cat's) are red. Bright-red holes. The snap was obviously taken by some genius who didn't know how to fix red-eye.

I never met my grandpa. Mom wouldn't let him in the house. I think there was a bit of history between them. No loss, he doesn't look like he was a lot of laughs.

I get my laptop and update the physical characteristics of snapshot number two: The Target. He's taking shape. Lucky Mr X is a tall, thin guy with red eyes and no sense of humour who loves cats. Lucky Grummer!

I join Grummer and Mr du Plooy on the veranda. His fingers are clenching the coffee mug like hairy, overcooked boerewors - swollen, meaty sausage fingers. Grummer's face is all pink and patchy. They're still stuck on the guava tree issue. I don't do conflict, so I leave them and go and check out the garden shacks — oh excuse me, Mr du Plooy, homes.

One of the buildings was a bedroom-cum-living-room-cum-everything else. The other was a kitchen (there's a place where a stove made a mark against the wall). The other is the bathroom (no bath but a rusty metal tub). The wallpaper is a collage of pictures from a magazine called *Scope*. And there's an old photo of two kids on the wall above a rotting mattress. One dark-looking girl and a whitish-looking boy.

Mr du Plooy and Grummer are still at it when I get back. They finally agree to disagree until Round Two. In the meantime Grummer says she'll chat to the neighbours about putting a pipe for the leiwater through their garden.

I watch Mr du Plooy off the property. He's

built like a tank and before he leaves he makes a turn into one of the shacks. He nearly takes his head off at the doorway. Ha-ha.

He emerges a bit later with a piece of paper in his hand. Shoot me dead for being a liar, but I swear it's the photo of the two kids. He takes a last look around the garden, checking out all the guava trees and then roars off in his four by four.

Over supper I raise my action plan for tomorrow. I do it carefully, 'cos I don't want to alert Grummer to the strategy.

"I feel the need ..." (yes, I say that) "I feel the need to pray, Grummer."

Grummer says she also feels the need to pray. She needs the Lord's help in dealing with Mr du Plooy. "I've never met a person so ... so ... otherwise," Grummer says. "I'm not used to dealing with difficult men. Your grandfather always used to know exactly how to deal with these sorts of people. He could always shout the loudest."

I add another quality to The Target snapshot: Bully.

Before Grummer suggests we hold hands and do the prayer thing, I suggest church. The Anglican Church has a nine o'clock service tomorrow morning and we can go together. Grummer looks pleased. "Your mother never wanted to go to church with her father and me. We will have a lovely time," she says.

Yes, we will, I agree. Project: Pulling for Grummer is entering a critical phase. Get ready to meet The Target.

ETA: Sunday 7:00 a.m. GMT.

Part Two

Chapter 8

IT'S 5:35 A.M. GMT. I put on my church clothes: pants (black), T-shirt (black) and boots (black). I discipline my hair severely with hairbands (black), put on my shades (black) and brush my teeth (twice). I'm now ready to meet my new grandpa.

I cast a critical eye over Grummer. She's gone for a navy-blue jacket and skirt with a red scarf around the neck. She looks like an air hostess. I tell her she looks very nice. She looks at my Sunday best, sighs and says nothing.

We walk to St Paul's Anglican Church together. Everybody's out walking. Old ladies walking their old men. Young men walking their old dogs. I keep a sharp eye out for thin old men with red eyes walking their cats. My luck's out.

We get there way too early, like half an hour. Grummer says she likes to prepare herself before a service. We take seats in the third row and Grummer kneels and prays. I play a few hands of poker on my cellphone and get my best score ever.

I look around and do a quick assessment of potential targets. Seven kids sit in the front row. I figure they're related 'cos the three girls wear dresses made from the same material. The oldest kid is about nine. I guess their parents are at home having a Sunday morning zizz. Let's face it, day care isn't cheap.

There are only two other customers present in the church. They sit very close to each other and giggle and hold hands. They're probably doing their attendance quota before they're allowed to get married.

I keep the faith; there's always the minister.

He comes up a little short of the key characteristics. He's like one metre forty, about eighty-five years old, with a set of clicking teeth, a hairy, grey top lip, a grey Alice band to keep a mop of grey hair our of his eyes and a grey dress. He's a she and her name is Pastor Hettie Druiwe.

We're ten minutes into the show when I figure it's time we cut our losses. I catch Grummer's attention and give her a sign — the finger across the throat. Grummer adjusts her red scarf and smiles back at me.

Pastor Aitch keeps us at it for three hours. We sing, we clap and we pray. We do it all in Afrikaans. And then Pastor Aitch tells us about this guy called *Johannes die Doper*, who lived in a desert. And I think of Mom and calculate that she's been without a dop for two days. Old John the Baptist didn't have a drink for forty days and Mom's got twenty-six more to go.

Pastor Aitch doesn't allow us to just sit and listen. Just when I think my bum's finally found a comfortable spot on the pew, she gets us to get on our knees. There's no warning, she just screeches, "*Gat op jou knieë!*"

We do this about twelve times in every hour.

It's like a high-intensity aerobics class. After the sermon, we sing, we clap and pray some more.

At the end of it all, Pastor Aitch comes and introduces herself. She gives us a register and asks us to sign our names.

"Are yous from England?" she asks Grummer. She thinks we're tourists. Grummer tells her where we live.

Pastor Aitch says, "Oh." And she makes big eyes at us. She says very few of the local white people come and worship with the coloured people. "It's still very us and them," she tells us and she takes Grummer's pale, speckly hand in her brown, leathery one and shakes it again.

"I knew the people who used to live by your place," Pastor Aitch tells Grummer. "They were also churchgoers. They grew the best quinces in the dorp."

Grummer and Pastor Aitch get talking and I wander outside. I watch people leave the other churches across the village green. I do some quick maths. I've got three more churches and three Sundays left in the holiday to get it right.

Grummer cooks Sunday lunch while I do some strategic analysis on my laptop. I adjust the information under Target Venues: doctor's rooms (one), churches (three).

I make another category: other. There must be other places where people with nice teeth who love God and went to university get together. Before I can do a brainstorm, Grummer calls me for lunch.

She's made a special effort. There are six bowls lined up on my side of the table. They each contain the following: pieces of lettuce, cherry tomatoes, chick-peas, two boiled eggs, tuna, and the last has sliced cucumber.

"Look, Beatrice. I've made it just as you like it. You will eat properly today? Say you will?" she pleads.

I say, "You will" and Grummer shakes her head at me like I've hurt her feelings.

She has two plates on her side of the table: a roast chicken and a mixed, dressed salad. She waits for the one o'clock news and then we eat.

She tells me that one of the people who used to

live on our property is still alive. Well, just. He's ninety years old and lives in the coloured township on the other side of the village. The township is called "Die Skema" or "The Scheme".

It's the name the authorities gave it when they came up with a scheme to chuck all the coloured people out of the village and take their land. And the name stuck. It stinks too. Grummer says it was daylight robbery! And she repeats it again in a voice with capital letters: DAYLIGHT ROBBERY!

I'm eating the yellow part of the egg (I don't like the white) and wondering where exactly Grummer's history lesson is going. She finally gets to the point: "Pastor Hettie has invited me to Die Skema to attend a prayer group of a few of her parishioners who are also bereaved," she says.

Ching-Ching! Now here's something I can work with. A group of singles getting all close up and personal with each other in an enclosed space. Holding hands, praying and comforting each other. I couldn't have planned things better. I give Grummer ten out of ten for initiative. If I hadn't had yellow egg all over my teeth I would've given her a big smile as well. I nod encouragingly instead.

After the prayer meeting, Pastor Hettie's going to take her to visit Mr September, Grummer tells me. I nearly choke on a chick-pea with excitement. A date! Already! My Grummer really is a dark horse.

"I want to talk to him about the guava trees and the quince trees ... before I make the decision to remove them all ... I don't want to do more wrong."

Okay, I get it. Grummer's going to see the old guy who used to live here. I don't like it one little bit. I mean he's so way out of the age range. He'll be dead before the honeymoon.

Conserve your energy, Grummer. FOCUS!

Grummer does. On two faces that are peering around the doorway.

"Hullooooo," says one of the faces. The face has a big red nose. My radar says Boozer. Grummer gets up from the table and greets The Neighbours.

Chapter 9

THE NEIGHBOURS ARE Mr and Mrs Thomas Phillips. They live in the house behind us.

"I can see *everything* that goes on in your home. Right into the little girl's bedroom. She's always *busy* on her computer. Working on a *secret* project, hey? Am I right, am I?" says Mrs Thomas Phillips, whose name turns out not to be Thomas at all; it's Candice.

Great. I make a mental note to increase security.

Grummer offers them tea. Mr Phillips checks his watch and he makes a joke about it being a little too early for the "other".

They take normal tea. So I make a pot of rooibos for me and Grummer and a pot of no-name brand special for the Phillipses.

"You *must* call us Tom and Candy," Mrs Phillips tells me when I take the tea onto the veranda. I tell them they *must* call me Beatrice.

Candy likes to place an emphasis on certain words in a sentence. When she does it, she bares her teeth and makes her mouth very wide. I can see she had something fleshy for lunch. Gross!

Candy asks me what I want to be when I grow up. I tell her I want to be tall. Grummer gives me a narrow-eyed look. I wink back behind my shades. Okay, Grummer, I'll play nice.

Tom runs a small antique shop (he calls it an "anteekee shoppee") in Hermanus, aimed at the weekend visitors from Cape Town.

"It's amazing what you can pick up in the countryside for *practically nothing*," Candy tells us.

"It's a cash business of course," Tom says. He taps his soggy nose as he lets us in on his little tax dodge. Poor Tom's got a bit of a cold. He's sure he picked it up in the dentist's rooms last week when he was having a crown fixed.

"The dentist is treating all sorts of people these days," he says. "A different sort of person, if you know what I mean? You take your life in your hands going in there."

I take a photo of Tom with my cellphone and upload it to my laptop. I do a little work in Photoshop and enlarge his nose. It looks like a sunburnt prickly pear. There are about seven bristles to each enlarged pore. It's one of my finest pieces of work. I send it to my two and only friends back home, captioned "Still-life of a nose in the countryside". They text me back that they love it too much.

Grummer tells Tom and Candy about the irrigation system she plans to put into the garden. She asks them if she can run a pipe down the side of their property so she can get the leiwater feed. She tells them she's not sure how it works, precisely.

Tom tells her, precisely, in between dribbling tea on his shirt, how it works. The leiwater was originally used to irrigate the vegetable gardens grown by coloured people in the middle of the twentieth century.

"*They're* not here any more and *we* still get the water. And it's for *practically nothing*. We only pay twenty ronts a month," Candy says, putting in her five cents' worth.

"Not that we grow *vegetables* of course. But, let's face it, you can't grow an English country garden without *lots* of water," Candy says.

Candy says Grummer just *has* to get rid of the guava trees. "*All* the starving kids from Die Skema will come and steal the fruit if you don't. It's *impossible*," she says.

I'm starting to like these people very much (not).

Candy says she will be *dee*lighted to accommodate Grummer's leiwater pipe. Tom asks Grummer who's putting in the irrigation system. When Grummer tells him, Tom tells Grummer what he thinks (precisely).

"Old Du Plooy's not a bad sort, as Afrikaners go. A bit too familiar with the coloureds," he says, and Candy pulls down her mouth knowingly.

The Phillipses are from England — Milton Keynes. They moved to South Africa thirteen years ago and bought in the village, for *practically nothing*, Candy says. Property prices, especially for land by the river, have now just gone *through the roof*.

I'm about to go through the roof, my head's hurting so badly. But the Phillipses stay and stay. And then they stay some more.

Candy asks Grummer what she's been up to. Grummer tells them that she got the house cleaned by the fairies. Candy says she has a girl from Die Skema. "You have to watch them *all the time*. I turn my back for *one second* and she's at the sugar. But labour's very cheap in these parts. She costs *practically nothing*. I'll lend her to you," she offers generously.

Grummer says she couldn't possibly accept. No, she simply couldn't. And she flaps her hands around madly like there's a bad smell in the air.

"You just can't get reliable labour this time of year," Tom says, stroking his nose. "They all go home to their tribal villages in the Transkei for Christmas."

The Phillipses miss Milton Keynes *awfully*. I think Milton Keynes misses them *awfully* and they should go back there. Fast.

Grummer tells Tom and Candy about the church service we attended and about meeting Pastor Hettie. Candy nearly falls off her chair laughing. "Oh, don't tell me you went to church this *morning*. Oh, my dear, that's the *wrong service*. It's for the *coloureds* from Die Skema. You're supposed to go in the *evenings* for the *white* service." And Candy and Tom shriek like a pair of psychos.

I've reached the conclusion that Tom and Candy will not be on my new best friend list. I'm about to email an anonymous complaint to the tax man about a certain Thomas Phillips, previously of Milton Keynes, Yoo Kay, when Candy finally says something interesting. I catch the tail end: "… and we meet at seven o'clock every Thursday night at one of the member's homes. It's very *informal* of course and we spend *more* time talking about each other than *books*, but it's *very* jolly."

Grummer says she belongs to a book club in Pee-Eee. She would love to attend one during the holidays. She's running out of decent books to read.

"And there are some really *super* people. One or two elderly gentlemen and a few younger ladies," says Candy.

Ka-ching! A book club. Of course! I make a mental note to update the Target Venue list.

Candy promises to discuss Grummer's holiday honorary membership with the other members and says she'll let Grummer know. "I think they will absolutely *jump* at you," she says. "We are bored to *death* of each other. And I'm so *sick* of the same old food everyone cooks. It will be a *lovely* change to have it in your home."

I think the Phillipses give up on Grummer ever offering them something decent to drink, 'cos at about 3:45 p.m. GMT, Tom announces that it's time to go.

"They seem pleasant enough people," Grummer says, clearing away the tea things.

Yeah, absolute charmers, Grummer.

She catches my eye. She holds my look for a second and then turns away. "I'm sure they mean well. Never judge a book by its cover, Beatrice," she says. But she looks cross. Like I've caught her in a lie. But I haven't said a word. Not one.

Grummer says she's going for her walk. She has her pre-breakfast walk and her pre-supper walk. She takes an hour's exercise every day. No more, no less.

I update my project file. I add two items to Target Venues: singles' prayer meetings, book club meetings (Thursdays). Things are happening fast. I am making progress!

Chapter 10

I'M SUSPENDED IN a hammock among the quince trees at the bottom of the garden, having a lovely time. I'm on talk-show radio in Detroit, America, the Yoo Ess of Aye.

The topic of the show is "What do you want for Christmas?" It's a completely lame topic, but it's the first time I've managed to use the technology that allows me to dial across the seas at the cost of a local call. I caught the show online and here I am, speaking to the American people. Yee-ha!

I've already ordered a leg wax from Santa in my best Valley Girl accent and the lady wants to know what else I want in my Christmas stocking. I tell her I want my Mom to get out of rehab so I can leave this dump. The lady moves on fast.

I'm just about to mention how I want a sober, professional, God-fearing geriatric for Grummer so I'll never have to see her again, when the topic of the talk-show pitches. I kill the call.

I've been used as a guinea pig all day. First, it was the steak casserole. Then the fish curry, and now Grummer's at my side doing a reverse Oliver Twist impersonation with a bowl of chicken tetrazzini.

"Just taste the sauce, Beatrice. You don't have to eat a whole spoon. Just a small lick," she begs, dipping into the pasta and chicken.

I swallow hard and taste some. I declare it an absolute winner.

"But you said that about the other two. Decide for me please, dear. Which dish should I serve tonight?"

Grummer looks so pathetic, I make the final decision. I tell her she should serve all three. They're all winners.

It's Grummer's big night. In approximately two hours, five book-loving people will arrive at our home to discuss the flavour of the month: *The Da Vinci Code*.

Grummer's "To Do" list has had six items on it for the past three days:

1. Read *The Da Vinci Code*
2. Prepare points for discussion
3. Cater
4. Clean
5. Arrange bookshelves
6. Get Beatrice to read *The Da Vinci Code*

That last point got me worried. The only books I've read in the past five years are technology and cellphone manuals. But I download the audio version of Dan Brown's book and listen to the first and last chapters. I read a couple of reviews off a book website and then update myself on the latest views from a couple of the million blogs on the subject. I come away with a few insights.

The first is that, according to the book, Jesus

and I have the same strategy. He also went fishing in the church pond to catch himself a nice religious girl. The second is that Jesus was a bachelor for a good thirty years before he pulled Mary. I've only got three weeks left to pull for Grummer and she's twice his age, so time's a bit of a factor. But I, too, can be patient. The third insight is that the Catholic Church is not a big fan of the marriage. In fact, Jesus kept it rather quiet until this Dan Brown character blew the whistle on him. I don't think Grummer needs this sort of aggro when she gets hitched again, so I delete the Catholic Church from my Target Venue list. I'm down to a shortlist of two churches: Methodist and Dutch Reformed.

Grummer calls me from the garden and asks me to smarten up before the guests arrive. So I take off my jeans (black) and T-shirt (black) and put on another pair of jeans (black) and another T-shirt (black).

I go and help Grummer set the table and prepare the snacks. I put 475 peanuts in one bowl and 192 pretzels in another. I check the bookshelves.

I spent a whole day arranging them into subject matter and then alphabetical order. They look lovely.

I'm folding the final creases into the napkins when The Neighbours arrive. Candy's *so excited* to be here. Tom's ticking. His nose looks like the inside of a pomegranate. He puts a bottle of wine (Chardonnay) on the table.

"I like red myself, but I thought you might like the white," he says to Grummer.

Boooiiiiing! News Flash! I can see the headline in the *Village Voice*: "Book Club Meeting Bombs as Mavis Wellbeloved hosts Dry Evening."

Grummer looks a little tense. Our house doesn't do booze. Our house faces a night of shame. I tell Grummer I'll be right back.

I shove my principles into my sock drawer and grab one of the bikes from the garage. I haven't ridden one of these things in five years, but, as they say, it's like riding a bicycle.

I see the green robot flashing outside the pubbingrill. It's happy hour and the place is buzzing.

There's a cross lady standing over a table, shouting at a man who's got seven empty Black Label beer bottles lined up in front of him. "Here you are again! Drinking all the money. Come home before I klap you all the way to Cape Town!" she screams, threatening to hit him. And the men around the bar look and laugh.

I catch Toffie in the kitchen slicing lemons.

I don't have any time for small talk. "Toffie. Give me wine," I say.

He gives me a reproachful look. "Ag no, Beat, man. I can't do that. You're underage. But hows about a Fanta?"

I take the knife out of his hand. I do a quick calculation of how long it would take to slice and dice Toffie into a million pieces. Too long. Perhaps another time. I give him the low-down in five clipped sentences: Grummer hosting book club. Don't have booze. They want booze. Face shame. Need wine fast.

Toffie gets it. He's not as slow as he looks. "Ag, Beat, man. Why didn't you say so in the first place?"

He goes around the back of the bar and comes back with a bag containing six bottles of wine. Three red, two white and one rosé.

"What you doing tomorrow?" he asks. "I've got this place I go to and want you to come." He holds the bag of wine tightly against his chest and waits for me to answer.

There are times in one's life when one has to do unpleasant things, like peeling onions, cleaning up vomit and putting out the garbage. This is one of those times. I say through my teeth that I'll see him in the morning then — and I grab the wine.

I get back home as the last guest arrives. Grummer's serving apple juice and everyone's eyeing Tom's Chardonnay with mean eyes. I give Grummer the wine and get some glasses.

"Beatrice, you're a good girl," Grummer says and she squeezes my shoulders.

Whatever.

Candy's *puffing* smoke out her nose and *flicking* ash on the carpet. So I get some ashtrays. Everyone else grabs their bags and lights up. Except for the one guy.

He stands next to Grummer and he's sipping apple juice. He's showing her a passage from the Bible and then he points to a page in *The Da Vinci Code*. He brushes a grey curl off his forehead as he makes a point. Grummer nods in agreement and smiles at him.

Ka-ching!

Chapter 11

EVERYONE WENT HOME. Finally. When they did, Grummer burnt lemon-scented candles to get the stink of cigarette smoke out of the house and then coughed all night. She's allergic.

This morning I'm sitting on the veranda with my laptop, typing up a report on the book club meet. Grummer's sipping tea and watching the honeybirds play in the Lion's Ear flowers. She's ticking off all the birds she sees in her *Roberts Bird Guide*. She likes to keep track.

My report says:

Five guests arrived at approximately 5:00 p.m.

GMT. They were Mr and Mrs Thomas Phillips, otherwise known as Tom and Candy. There was Gill Goldman, a forty-something female with big breasts. The fourth was Eric Stephenson, a chain smoker, thirty-nine (although with diminishing life expectancy), with smelly breath and stress acne. The last guest was Mr Alan Rodderick, aka Mr Perfect.

My report continues with a detailed description of Mr Perfect, a summary of which says:

He dresses like a Gap model. He speaks like a cellphone advert. He eats nice and neat. (He is a piscatarian — loved Grummer's fish curry.) He's the librarian in Hermanus and studied at both Cape Town and Stellenbosch universities (got a Bee Aye from Yoo Cee Tee and Honours in Library Studies from Stellenbosch Uni). He's fifty-nine, unmarried and goes to church (St Luke's Anglican in Hermanus). He has hair — but only on his head — and absolutely doesn't drink (alcohol).

I enter his name under The Target. I assess my timeline. We've been here a week and I've made progress! Three more weeks to go. I am feeling pretty chuffed with myself. Mr Perfect's coming for lunch on Sunday after church. I set it up. This is how I did it: while Tom, Candy and the other non-targets drank their way through Toffie's wine supply and talked about who was stealing whose *leiwater* and who got fined cheating on the water restrictions, Grummer and Mr Perfect chatted about *The Da Vinci Code*.

They both agreed that Mr Brown had perhaps been selective in his use of material and that poor Jesus never really made it with Mary. Which is bad news, considering he's over 2,000 years old and still single. I should give him a couple of tips on book clubs.

And then Mr Perfect ("call me Alan — with one el") asked me who my favourite author was. I mentioned a couple of the Google and Nintendo geeks, but Alan didn't seem to know their work. I spotted the gap and took it. "Alan." (Ahem.) "Alan," I said, "could you perhaps recommend a couple of good authors. My mom's not too big on books, so I feel a little lost." Ag, shame!

And so it was agreed. Alan's coming for lunch

and bringing me some books. And he's bringing his housemate Greg, an old guy of about sixty-two who runs the Hermanus bookshop. Two book-lovers at one sitting. Grummer will be spoilt for choice.

I'm tapping out the last triumphant line of my report when Toffie arrives. I grind my teeth and get my bike. Grummer asks about lunch. Toffie says it's fine, he's packed a picnic. Oh, yippee!

Toffie takes me to this place on the river just outside the dorp. It's a deserted, walled reservoir. He's put in some doors and windows, and there's a sheet to make like a sort of roof. He calls it his den. I call it a dump.

He's got a whole lot of stuff in a box hidden in a hole in the wall: his stamp collection, with his precious Penny Black (yawn), his baby teeth and some old South African coins. He calls it his treasure. I call it so totally yesterday.

Toffie says it's time for the picnic and we go down to the river's edge. He spreads out a blanket and unpacks his rucksack. I'm not sure the day can get any worse, but it does.

There are beef sandwiches, lamb sandwiches and ham sandwiches. I tell Toffie I don't do meat.

"Ma said you wouldn't, so she packed you a special lunch," he says and waves some peanut butter sandwiches in my face. Real special.

I whip out my cellphone and go online. I google peanut butter sandwiches and learn that Bill Gates, Madonna and Lance Armstrong eat them. Swell.

I watch a huge red snake swim lazily across the river to the clump of reeds at the other side. I point it out to Toffie.

"I call him Rooi Duiwel. He's always here," Toffie says.

I eat a peanut butter sandwich. It tastes like brain power, artistic genius and sweat. I try to ignore the bread taste and eat three more. Toffie finishes seven sandwiches, makes a big burp and goes and swims. He heads out towards the reeds and I cross my toes and hope Red Devil the snake finishes him off.

I fall asleep on the blanket and I dream that Melinda Gates is chasing me on a bike, singing,

"Give me back Bill's brain food."

I wake up with Toffie shaking half the river all over me. His face is inches from mine.

"Jis, Beat, but your nose is red. You've caught the sun," he says.

I tell him it's time I caught my ride home and leave him by the river.

Grummer's out walking, so I go and check out my nose. It looks like I'm related to Tom of The Neighbours. I cover my face with cold cream.

Over supper Grummer tells me she's looking forward to going to church with me again at St Paul's on Sunday morning. I say no can do. Grummer must appreciate that the morning service is a dead end. And, anyway, Mr Perfect's in the bag. There's no more need to hit the churches.

"Grummer, we've got people for lunch at one o'clock. We don't have time for morning church," I say. Grummer says she's preparing the night before. It's cold pickled fish and salads for lunch. Can't wait.

"Grummer," I say, choosing another tactic, "Grummer, I battle with the Afrikaans. I need to hear the Lord's word in English."

Grummer's eyes narrow with suspicion. She gives me a skeef look and says it had appeared to her that I had enjoyed the sermon last week.

I give it my best: "I liked the fact that John the Baptist went to the desert for rehab, but how could he fall off the wagon and go back to drinking when Jesus arrived? How could he, Grummer?" I say.

Grummer says we'll go to the Anglican service in the evening.

I say sure thing.

I think: Mr Alan Rodderick. I think: Mrs Mavis Rodderick.

It is a sure thing.

Chapter 12

IT'S SUNDAY AFTERNOON and I'm lying by the river at Toffie's den. I'm watching Rooi Duiwel sunning himself by the reeds and I'm wondering if he's going to peel as badly as my nose.

I'm also thinking that I'm a category-one loser. All in capitals: CATEGORY-ONE LOSER. Toffie and his pals should make me eligible for life membership. I deserve to have BIG L tattooed onto my forehead and put on a current affairs television programme like *Carte Blanche* to tell the viewers: "The Story of a Loser".

It goes like this: at approximately 10:58 a.m.

GMT, Mr Perfect and his housemate Greg arrived at Chez Wellbeloved for Sunday lunch. Alan, with one el, brought some books for Beatrice Wellbeloved. Present location: propping up the broken leg of the desk in her bedroom.

Greg, with two gees, brought Mrs Mavis Wellbeloved an orchid. Yellow. Present location: pride of place on the dining-room table.

The widow Wellbeloved was looking understated and casual (read dowdy), dressed in Capri pants (navy blue) with cotton shirt (white). Beatrice Wellbeloved was similarly casually attired in long pants (black) with matching T-shirt.

The lunch proceeded in an atmosphere of congenial jollity. Discussion topics included gardening, God, adult fiction. And then gardening, God, children's fiction.

The television camera could not have missed, as the keen-eyed Beatrice Wellbeloved should not have missed, how Alan and Greg looked at each other throughout lunch. Nor could the camera have missed the nurturing way Greg spooned clotted cream onto Alan's bowl of berries.

However, should the camera have failed to capture these intimate gestures, the dialogue at the end of the meal, when Greg and Alan had driven off in their white Mini Cooper, would have put the *Carte Blanche* viewers in the picture.

"What a super couple, don't you think, Beatrice?" Mrs Wellbeloved said to her red-nosed granddaughter.

"Couple?" said Chico the Clown to Mrs Wellbeloved.

"Yes, they've been together for thirty-five years. Goodness me, that's almost as long as your grandfather and I were together," said Mrs Wellbeloved, taking a cunningly hidden wad of tissues from her bra strap and dabbing her eyes.

While washing up the lunch dishes Mrs Wellbeloved commented further: "If your grandfather had been around, he would never have allowed Alan and Greg into the house. He always saw things so black and white. There was right and wrong. And in his eyes, Greg and Alan's special friendship would have been wrong," Grummer said, putting away the dessert bowls.

Exactly! Grandpa and me would have agreed on this. It's wrong. It's not the way it should be. Alan is Mr Perfect. And now I get it that he's Greg's Mr Perfect. It's a crime.

Grummer can see how cross I am. She gives me this long talking-to about how the Lord loves everybody and that prejudice is an ugly thing. Grummer's getting me wrong. She forgets that Mom owns an advertising company. There are a zillion Gregs and Alans and Betties and Barbaras working for Mom. But I never wanted any of them to marry Grummer. What a waste of time and FOCUS!

The television camera zooms in and freezes on the face of The Loser and then the credits appear.

I text my two and only friends back home the details of my new loser status. They don't respond. Hey, I can't blame them. Who wants to hang with people like me and Toffie in the Loser Club?

Toffie arrives just as I'm thinking about offering myself up to Rooi Duiwel as a living sacrifice. I don't know how he knew I was here. I suppose losers can smell their own.

"Hey, Beat, want to swim?" he asks.

I tell him I want to drown myself.

He offers me a peanut butter sandwich.

I eat four.

He asks me what I'm thinking about.

I tell him I'm thinking that I'm related to the Son of God. I think my dad ditched me just after I was born to protect me from the Catholic Church and their secret organisation. He left me and Mom so that the Holy Grail, me, the bloodline of the Holy Trinity, would survive undetected by Silas the albino monk.

Toffie's shocked. He says Silas works for his ma in the bar, but Silas is black. Not albino. And he's no monk; he's married. He lives in one of the shacks in the squatter settlement above Die Skema for people from the Transkei. They call the settlement Die Trein or The Train 'cos it snakes like a train up the hillside.

I tell Toffie he's an idiot. Then I tell him all about *The Da Vinci Code*.

Toffie cans himself laughing. "But Beat, everybody knows that Jesus wasn't a ladies' man."

I'm furious with Toffie. I've had it up to here with happy bachelors and miserable moffies. I've had enough of Mr Perfect and his super housemate Greg. And I tell Toffie too.

"Ag, Beat," Toffie says. "You mustn't be so prejudiced. My uncle's a moffie and he's okay. Gay people are fine, really." I want to hit him.

It's funny how people can look like something and be something else. I tell him I never knew Mr Potato, our plumber, his uncle, was gay. Toffie says he didn't know either. But his father's other brother, his Uncle Koos, definitely is. He lives in an artists' colony in Greytown and works with pastels.

I try it on and get it. Koos Appel. Appel Koos. Apricot! The apricot in the potato and pineapple family. I feel so much better. Everything fits as it should.

I tell Toffie that I think his family's mad. That they're all crazy with their fruity, vegetable, silly names. And Toffie agrees and says that the thought of his crazy family makes him feel very happy.

And I feel very unhappy. 'Cos I know that unless

I pull a nice old man for Grummer, I'm going to be stuck with her and people like Toffie until I'm old enough to buy my first legal Lotto ticket. And 'cos I'm feeling so mad, I tell him about the project.

Toffie laughs at me. "Ag, Beat, man. You should've asked. I know all the old ballies in this dorp. Ask me for a list of the old men and I'll give it to you. I'll get your ouma fixed up in no time," he says and then he takes off his T-shirt and goes and swims with Rooi Duiwel.

I go and sit on the jetty and take off my takkies. I put my feet in the water and they feel wet. And I think about how Mom always says that the key to successful project management is leveraging the talents of employees. And I look through my shades at Toffie flipping around in the water and I think he's about as bad as it will get.

At the end of it all, I blame the sugar in the peanut butter sandwiches. But today my feet feel cool. And I decide: okay, Toffie, you're on board Project: Pulling for Grummer. We start at nine o'clock.

Tomorrow!

Chapter 13

IT'S TOMORROW AND I want to fire Toffie already. I've been waiting by the den since 7:00 a.m. GMT. It's now 7:34 a.m. GMT, and for anyone who knows time zones and can do basic maths, that's more than half an hour after nine o'clock. I hate tardy staff.

Toffie arrives on his bike at 7:45 a.m. GMT with something rolled under his arm. It's a map of the village with every house marked off in a square. He took it off his aunty who works for the estate agency. I decide to give Toffie a second chance.

Toffie sticks the map on the wall. "Okay, look here, Boss, there are …" I do a quick scan. I tell him I see 827 homes in the dorp.

"Nope. There are 812 homes and fifteen businesses," Toffie says. I want to fire him even more.

I like to work methodically. We start at the first row of houses and he tells me exactly who's living there. When we hit a potential target, he makes a big cross over the square with a red pen; with a blue pen, we cross off all of the squares inhabited by single women or married couples.

After two rows of houses, Toffie says he needs to check something out. So we get on the bikes and go to a row of houses and he makes sure that the occupants are who he thinks they are.

Toffie has a routine. He knocks on the door and asks the person something dumb like "Is your husband in?" And if the answer is no, he asks, "When will he be coming home?" And if a man answers the door he asks the same question about the wife.

If people ask the reason for his stupid questions

he gives the same answer: "The pubbingrill's having a skop on Saturday night and my ma wants to know if you want to buy tickets."

And he sells a ticket for the pubbingrill party every time. And then he gets me to do it too. His mom is giving him two rand for every ticket he sells. He gives me one of those rands for every ticket I sell. Over the next four days we do a lot of this checking by going door to door, and we sell a lot of tickets. I'm not sure who's employing who any more.

Toffie takes his rights as a worker seriously. He says that he needs to be properly equipped. So I tell him I'll get some more red and blue pens. He shakes his head and says the internal communication system of the company is vrot. I tell him nonsense, it's his work ethic that's rotten. Then he goes swimming for the rest of the afternoon until I give him my spare cellphone. I draw the line when he asks me to pay for his airtime.

On the fifth day Toffie goes on strike. He says it's too hot to work and, anyway, it's the Day of Reconciliation. He won't work on a public holiday. I say I won't sell any more tickets. He says he'll work after he's had a swim. I tell him Rooi Duiwel's waiting. He says he wants to swim with me. I tell him I don't have a costume. He fetches his sister's old one. I tell him I'd rather eat raw buffalo intestines than swim in that costume. He says he's resigning and he's taking his tools with him. He fetches the map from the den and starts walking away with The Targets. *My* targets.

I get changed into Adore Appel's costume. I look adorable (not). I keep myself covered with a towel until I reach the jetty and then I jump in. I swim. And then I swim some more. And then I tell Toffie to fetch my sunscreen (factor 50$^+$) from the den and when he's gone I jump out of the water and wrap myself in the towel.

I sit on the bank of the river and I feel tiny ants biting my skin. But when I take off my towel I don't see ants.

Toffie comes back with my factor 50$^+$ and stares at my legs.

"Jis, Boss," he says, "look at your legs."

I look at them and I see these white things covered in hair. And I hate Toffie for looking. And I hate Mom for never getting it together to take me for a wax.

Toffie reaches over and flicks white crystals away with his fingers. I hate Toffie more for touching my legs.

"The river's all choked up. In a couple of days they'll break through the sand bank by the lagoon and then the salt will get washed away to the sea," he says, licking his finger.

I scratch the salt crystals off my legs and cover them in cream. I tell Toffie it's time to work. He lays the map on the ground. There are thirty-two red crosses on the map. We go through each one and in the first round we cross off fifteen. All fifteen are single men under the age of fifty. Too young.

During the second round we knock off six more names. These are all single men over the age of seventy. Too old. Toffie says there are eleven names left. I say, yeah, like duh!

We disqualify another three names on the basis

of their professional status. One drives a soft-serve combi. Toffie says the ice-cream van is a clever front — he's actually a perlemoen smuggler. Very professional. I say I don't think smuggling abalone is so professional.

The others are a painter (walls not art) and a plumber (Mr Dreyer). Toffie says there's nothing wrong with plumbers. I say I'm very fond of plumbers personally, but the client wants a professional man. Toffie says I don't know what my Grummer really wants. I say I want to move on to the eight finalists.

I try to employ the next criterion on the lucky eight, and Toffie just gives up on me. "If you're looking for an old man who doesn't drink in this dorp, you're wasting your time, man, Beat. Everyone drinks here. There's nothing else to do."

I say we'll be guided by bodily hair. So we go and sell more tickets. I scratch two from the list after they say they already bought tickets in the morning when they were at the pubbingrill having a couple of toots or seven. I don't care what Toffie says, I think drinking so early in the morning is taking "nothing else to do" a bit too seriously. Dr Peter Waterford is still partying in Jozi, but my remaining one is adequately haired and I snap his photo with my cellphone.

Toffie comes back with four photos he took using his cellphone. I put three of the candidates out of their misery on the basis of extreme ugliness. Toffie says I'm ugly about ugly people. I say I'm ugly about ugly old men.

We put the uglies in the slush pile and we look at the three remaining names: Mr David Davis-Davis (senior school religious studies teacher aka the educated God-squadder), Dr Simon Fridjohn (veterinarian aka the professional animal lover) and Dr Peter Waterford (doctor aka the professional professional).

All bases covered.

Gotcha!

Chapter 14

I LOOK AT The Targets and I tell Toffie it's been swell, but all good things come to an end. If he could just turn in the cellphone and hand me the fifty-two rand he owes me for the tickets, I'll be on my way.

Toffie says that's just fine and what a pity me and Grummer don't have tickets for the pubbingrill skop.

I say that's cool bananas 'cos who needs a party when I've got the three names that'll take Grummer dancing down the aisle.

And Toffie says that's fine again and he gives me

back my spare cellphone and says it's a crime that two of the old fossils on the list will be dancing with some other nice old ladies at the pubbingrill tomorrow night while me and Grummer sit like wet farts at home.

Because, get this, Beatrice Wellbeloved, he says, Mr David Davis-Davis and Dr Simon Fridjohn each bought a single ticket from him the day before yesterday.

Toffie's got me. And so I give him back the cellphone and buy two tickets at one rand discount each for the pubbingrill skop.

I leave Toffie cutting bits of dry skin off his cracked heels with his penknife and go home.

Grummer's having lunch on the veranda with Mr du Plooy. I sit down and join them.

"Beatrice has been very busy cycling and swimming with her new friend Christoffel," Grummer says. "I've hardly seen her at all these past five days. Look how tanned and lovely she's looking."

I rush inside and look at myself in the mirror. A quick scan tells me I've got eleven freckles on my nose and seven on my cheeks. I want to cut my head off.

I go back to the veranda just as Grummer's dishing up the food: boerewors and mashed potatoes. Grummer and Mr du Plooy are arguing about the vegetable garden.

"But, Mrs Wellbeloved, even the queen of England grows cabbages among her roses. They keep the aphids away," says Mr du Plooy. I watch as he pours gravy all over his sausage and mash and mixes it up like a cement mixer. Sis!

"My husband's family came out of a world war where they grew vegetables just to survive. Derek (my late husband) always swore that he would never grow another vegetable," Grummer argues, looking all pink-cheeked.

Mr du Plooy eats his mash with the side of his knife and cuts his boerewors with a fork and shovels it down.

He's starting on the garden tomorrow. But they still haven't settled on the questions of the quince and guava trees and the demolition of the "homes".

After lunch, Pastor Hettie and Mr September are coming around to see the garden for the last time. Grummer says it was her idea. It'll help her decide what to do. I decide I've got plenty to do.

I get my laptop and open file Project: Pulling For Grummer. It hasn't been updated since the book club meet. I delete Alan Rodderick from The Target and put in the three new names. I imagine how Grummer takes to her three fiancés. I say the names out loud: Mrs Mavis Fridjohn. Yes! Mrs Mavis Waterford. Lovely! Mrs Mavis Davis-Davis. Nah! I sound like Mom after a bottle of vodka.

I call Toffie. He says he's at the video shop downloading *Shall We Dance?* for Adore and he'll call me back. I kick myself for giving him the URL of that Russian website.

When he finally calls, I ask him what's behind the David Davis-Davis thing. He tells me Mr Davis-Davis was originally plain Mr David Davis from the wrong side of the dorp. Then thirty years ago he met Ms Bridget Davis (no relation) from the right side of the village and they fell in love.

I'm finding this Romeo and Juliet saga very interesting (not) and I tell Toffie to get to the point. The point is that Ms Bridget Davis's snobby father would only allow his daughter to marry the low-life Mr David Davis if he would take the bride's family name and preserve the honourable line. So he became Mr David Davis-Davis. The union ended (sans children) three years ago when Mrs Bridget Davis-Davis was hit by a tractor overtaking a truck on the way to Hermanus.

I tell Toffie it's one of the worst stories I've ever heard in my life and it's just too bad but Mr David Davis-Davis will have to join the uglies in the slush pile. We'll get back to him if the other two targets crash.

Toffie says whatever. He has to download *Sleepless in Seattle* for his ma and can't talk. I shut the laptop and check out the action outside.

Grummer, Pastor Aitch, Mr du Plooy and a very old man (outside the target market) who Pastor Aitch calls Oom are wandering around the guava trees. I don't think the old man is Pastor Aitch's uncle, but that's what she respectfully calls him.

"*Kyk, seun. Kyk hierso,*" the old man says, and he's pointing at the thickest trunk of a very old guava tree at the edge of the garden. Mr du Plooy looks and smiles. There are some words carved on the tree: *K and G Forever 1966.*

"*Ek onthou.* Of course I remember that day," Mr du Plooy says and he puts his big (hairy) hand on the old man's shoulder. Mr du Plooy has a funny look on his face. But it looks like some of the things he's thinking aren't funny at all. And I don't feel like laughing either.

Mr du Plooy and Mr September go into one of the shacks and leave me and Grummer and Pastor Aitch to chatter outside.

Pastor Aitch is telling Grummer about this crèche she and the other ladies from Die Skema are trying to start for the Die Trein children, and Grummer sounds very interested. She says it sounds like a good cause. She would like to do her bit. And I don't say anything 'cos I'm so not interested. Not one little bit.

They finally come out of the shack and Mr September tells Grummer he found some things he wants to keep. Grummer sees that these things are some old photographs and she says of course.

I notice that there isn't the photo of two kids I saw before but I don't say anything, and Mr du Plooy doesn't say anything, and I think I know why: 'cos he nicked it when he was last here.

Mr du Plooy is looking very hot. His face is a big red tomato. Grummer offers to get him some cold water but he says, nonono, he'll be fine in a minute.

Pastor Aitch says she thinks we should pray about things and Mr du Plooy says he thinks he should leave and I say I think it's not a bad idea. We leave Grummer, Pastor Aitch and Mr September praying by the quince trees.

When Grummer comes inside she says we need to talk about tomorrow. And I say we definitely need to talk about tomorrow. Tomorrow is the night of the skop. Tomorrow is when she meets Dr Simon Fridjohn at the party. Let's talk, Grummer.

About tomorrow.

Chapter 15

WHEN I GO to bed on Friday night I enter the "talk about tomorrow" discussion in my file of some of my grossest conversations ever. It goes like this:

Beatrice says: "Grummer, the pubbingrill's having a dance tomorrow night."

Grummer replies: "Yes, Beatrice." Awkward silence.

Beatrice says: "I want to go." (And Beatrice thinks: I so do not want to go.)

Grummer asks: "Are you going to go on a date with Christoffel?"

Beatrice says: "It's a sort of date." (And Beatrice thinks: I'm so definitely not going on a date with Christoffel, or Toffie or any of his relatives. But you've got a date, Grummer, with Dr Simon Fridjohn.)

Grummer says: "I'm not sure if you're old enough for this sort of thing."

(Beatrice thinks: But you're old enough.) And Beatrice says: "But I badly want to go."

Grummer says: "I can't let you go out alone at night. It's not the right thing."

Beatrice says: "You're right, Grummer. I think you must come with me."

And then Grummer decides and says she'll come — but just for a short time. But we have to go shopping and buy "something pretty" to wear. I think that's an excellent idea. Grummer could do with something a little more jazzy. Her wardrobe really is on the dull side of dowdy.

Then Grummer has her turn to "talk about tomorrow". This also occupies a place of honour in my file of grossest conversations ever.

I don't say much. I just count the liver spots on

Grummer's hands as she talks on and on.

Here is a paraphrase of it: Grummer has a terrible "burden". It's all to do with that old man Mr September, who used to grow fruit and vegetables on this plot and then got chucked off the land in the olden days when apartheid was the big thing. Now tomorrow Grummer's going to ask (firmly ask) Mr du Plooy to rip up the last of his garden and she is feeling bad about it.

Why? Now this is the killer: "Mr September lost his wife shortly after they were forced to move to Die Skema. But he came back one night after the funeral and sprinkled her ashes in the garden ... among the quince trees," Grummer says.

I keep awake by concentrating on making my feet go numb. Then my ankles and then my calves. I move suddenly and it gives me this crazy, tingling feeling.

"Yes, I was also terribly moved by Mr September's story. You see, Beatrice, I scattered your grandfather's ashes in our rose garden at home. And whenever I see those roses, I imagine that there is something of your grandfather in those wonderful blooms," Grummer says. And she goes for one of those tissues she likes to hold captive in her bra strap.

Grummer's big dilemma is that she wanted to plant a garden that Grandpa would like — an English country garden full of hollyhocks and roses, elms and oaks — not rotten old fruit trees. Grummer asks me what I think.

I think it all sounds completely gross and boring. I also think Grummer must FOCUS! on her big date tomorrow. I say, "I think you must focus on what's really important. Like on real live people, not dead things."

Grummer sighs and smiles and she thanks me for being so wise.

The next morning we leave Mr du Plooy starting on the garden and head off to the big city of Hermanus to get "something pretty" for Grummer to wear to the skop.

We go to Foschini clothing store and Grummer picks out a red dress from the rack. I tell her it's a bit small. I don't want to be totally rude, but I also think red's a bit loud for someone her age.

I say the black one would be better. Grummer holds the red dress against me and says she thinks the size and colour are "just perfect". I take the dress and put it back on the rack. I tell Grummer I'm already sorted.

"I don't think so, Beatrice," Grummer says. "I can't have you going to your first dance dressed in trousers." And she takes the red dress off the rack again.

"And while we are here. Let's get you a decent bathing costume. I don't know where you picked up that thing you've been swimming in," Grummer says and she starts off in the direction of the costume rack.

I can be laid back. I know that there are times in one's life when one must just go with the flow. One must let things happen. One must take life as it comes. I know that this is definitely not one of those times.

I look at Grummer holding up a bikini and tell her I'll take the dress. I lure her past Aye Cee Kermans into Woolworths to pick out her outfit.

We make it back home just in time to meet Tom

and Candy weaving up the driveway. They're on their way back from a lunch at the brewery and want Grummer to make up a fourth tonight in a game of Rummikub.

"Not that we do a lot of *playing*. It's talk *mostly*. But it's *always* good fun," Candy says. She thinks it might be nice to have it at our house, for a *change*.

Grummer's says she's awfully sorry — not that I think she looks very sorry — but she's going to the dance at the pubbingrill.

Tom does his psycho laugh and Candy says, "Oh, you're *not*, Mavis. Not the *pubbingrill*. None of *our* sort goes *there*."

And Tom jabs Candy in the ribs and says they go there sometimes when everywhere else is closed and they need one for the road. Which reminds him … and he and Candy hit the road.

I tell Grummer I need to wash my hair (review my research) and she asks me what time Toffie's coming. We can all go together in her car when he arrives. I tell Grummer I'm meeting Toffie at the pubbingrill and Grummer titch-tiches and says

115

it's just not good enough; they never did things like that in her day.

So I get Toffie on his cellphone — correction: my cellphone — and I tell him he has to be my date for the skop; otherwise Grummer will be miffed. And her cross face is not going to get her skipping up the aisle.

Toffie doesn't play nice. He's still cheesed off at me for trying to confiscate his (my) cellphone and kick him off the project. "Nonono, Beat. No can do. You're the boss. It would be like … like too familiar. What would the rest of the staff think," he says and then he wets himself laughing. I tell him he's fired and he must come at seven o'clock. Precisely 5:00 p.m. GMT.

Toffie's having too much fun to stop. "Jis, Beat, you're forward. Don't you know it's the boy who has to ask the girl on the date? You must like me a lot, hey? Come on, say it."

I say nothing. Not even "it".

I hear him sigh. He says if I can't give him romance, then he'll take my cash. He says he'll see me at a quarter past seven after I use Mom's credit card and buy him 200 rands' worth of airtime.

I know Dr Simon Fridjohn's going to be worth every last cent. I know it, 'cos I've done my research.

Chapter 16

IT'S AMAZING WHAT you can find out when you email trusting institutions about job references. Dr Simon Fridjohn is sixty-one years old. He went to school at Bishops in Cape Town and did a science degree in the same city at Yoo Cee Tee, where he played tennis and hockey. He then took a veterinary degree and has been running a practice just outside the village for the past twenty years. He's unmarried and reads biographies of famous animals in his free time.

There's a photo of him on his school website with his life creed: "Simple Simon says, if you treat animals like people, they will behave like them."

He looks a bit young for sixty-one, but I suspect it's his old school photo.

Grummer knocks on my door and says it's nearly time to go. I brush my teeth four times and put the red dress on over a pair of jeans (black) and pull on a long T-shirt (black).

Grummer's done her hair. She put hot rollers in and then sprayed her curls so her hair's like a crash helmet. I tell her she looks lovely. She looks at me and sighs.

Toffie arrives and tells Grummer he likes her hairdo. He looks at me and laughs. "You sure clean up nice, Boss," he says and winks.

The green light on the robot outside the pubbingrill is on. Not that anyone needs telling that the place is open. People are on the pavement, inside the bar and standing around a fire in the back courtyard. Me and Grummer go outside 'cos she says she can't bear the cigarette smoke. Toffie follows and sticks to me like a leech. The dancing hasn't started and everyone's drinking and eating steaks and boerewors rolls. The smell of the sausage makes me feel sick and I go back inside.

I wonder how we're ever going to find Dr Simon Fridjohn. I check out the photo that Toffie took on his ticket-selling rounds: Dr Fridjohn's standing in his surgery, hugging a big, hairy dog. Or the dog's hugging him; I'm not sure. I can spot a rather freaky smile from under the dog's armpit. It's not a lot to go on.

I feel panicked. If I fail with Dr Simon Fridjohn I have to eat a double steak burger. That's the deal I made with my two and only friends back home. And they want a five-minute video clip of me doing it. The penalty for failure is harsh.

Grummer and Toffie come to find me, and Toffie introduces us to Adore. She's very friendly and says a lot of thank yous for the new stock of DVDs Toffie's been supplying her. They're selling like hot cakes. She says she's going to branch into music CDs next if I can give Toffie a good URL.

"The way things are going I'll be at Yoo Cee Tee next year," she says.

Grummer hears all this and looks at Adore. Her

eyes narrow and the line between her eyebrows deepens into a donga. That furrowed brow signals danger. She puts her hand on Adore's shoulder, to get her complete attention. "My girl. Would you steal a person's cellular telephone? Would you steal a person's handbag?" Grummer sounds like a bad anti-piracy advert.

Adore looks at Grummer's cross face and she figures the answer can't be yes. So she says no.

Grummer nods. "Of course not. What you are doing is piracy. And it's theft."

Adore says she has a copy of *The Last Temptation of Christ* which she can let Grummer have for cheap. The quality isn't so good and it looks like there's a snowstorm 24/7. But if she makes her eyes squint, Grummer can pretend it's a sandstorm. Which is fine because it's set in the Middle East, which is very sandy.

Grummer's eyes brighten. And then I see her lips move like she's making a prayer. And then she shakes her head. "No, Adore. No. It's not right. And if you carry on like this, the closest you will get to the University of Cape Town is

Pollsmoor prison."

Adore lowers her head and she says Grummer's right. But she was only trying to save for medical school. Grummer gets abnormally interested and tells us a very long story about how Grandpa had wanted Mom to be a doctor.

"But she left school and went overseas and came back with Beatrice," Grummer says. And she gives me a squeeze. I give her one back just to feel what Dr Simon Fridjohn will be feeling later on tonight. I think he'll be fine if he likes squishy flesh.

"Derek (my late husband) was very cut up about it. He had his heart set on Beatrice's mother becoming a doctor. He was a dentist, you know. He felt she had made the wrong choice. Sad really, because if he could see Beatrice today, he would know that she couldn't have chosen any other way." Grummer's going great guns for the Most Embarrassing Granny Oscar tonight. She goes on and on and on and we leave Adore having her ear chewed off.

Toffie finds his mom rinsing some glasses with

Silas. I check Silas out thoroughly. There's no trace of any albino patches on his hands and face, and Toffie gives me a told-you-so look.

Mrs Appel tells Toffie that Dr Simon Fridjohn is in the non-smoking dining room. She's making him a special soya burger 'cos he doesn't eat animals. I like Dr Simon Fridjohn more and more. Mrs Appel says she'll make me one too.

We tell her we'll also eat in the dining room and we grab Grummer away from Adore just as she's doing the closing chapter of "Derek's Big Disappointment".

"And so Derek and Beatrice's mother never spoke again. When I look back, it seems like such a waste of precious time."

I think Grummer's wasting precious time and we take her through to the dining room. I spot Dr Simon Fridjohn immediately. He's eating a big plate of salad and feeding scraps of soya burger to three cats under the table. We look around at the full dining room and then Toffie asks Dr Simon Fridjohn if we can join him. I'm so happy I decide to give Toffie a raise.

Dr Simon Fridjohn smells like antiseptic and he has very white hairless hands, like sterile gloves. He eats nice and doesn't talk between mouthfuls.

I'm celebrating victory when I notice Grummer's starting to itch. There are red welts on her arms and her neck looks like a turkey's. Then she starts sneezing all over Dr Simon Fridjohn, which I think is a bit too intimate for a first date. He doesn't seem to mind too much.

"Allergic are you?" he asks.

And Grummer tells him a long story about how she's allergic to animal fur and cigarette smoke and pollen and bees and mosquito bites. And so she goes on.

"Derek (my late husband) loved animals and at the time of his death he had three cats and two dogs. It was agony for me, but he insisted on having them. When he passed away, I had them put down," Grummer says.

I watch as Dr Simon Fridjohn nearly chokes on his salad and then how he gets up and leaves the dining room, taking the three cats with him.

"Oh dear," says Grummer, "did I say

something?"

You sure did, Grummer.

Grummer leaves us and goes and joins Mr du Plooy at the next table. He's wolfing down a steak and going for broke (double brandy and Coke).

I order a double steak burger and get Toffie to video me with the cellphone. He's telling me how I messed up with my research and saying isn't it funny that Grummer hates animals. And I think it's so not funny. I hate failing, it makes me sick.

Ching-Ching! I check the electronic diary on my cellphone and see that it's been two weeks since I arrived in the dorp. Two weeks have passed and I'm feeling sick.

I need a doctor!

Part Three

Chapter 17

GRUMMER'S STANDING BY the side of my bed looking very anxious. "I am not sure whether I should leave you on your own while I go to church, Beatrice," she says.

I groan and roll around on my bed, getting caught up in the mosquito net.

"Perhaps you ate something?" Grummer says.

Yeah, like a double steak burger. But that's not what's making me sick. Dr Peter Waterford's making me sick. He's back from Jozi and I need him. Grummer needs him.

I tell Grummer she can go off and do her

workout with Pastor Aitch; I'll survive.

Grummer says if I'm sure, and I say I'm very sure.

She asks me if I want her to leave the Sunday morning classical music special on and I tell her it's fine, I like it. I like the adverts they play in between the music.

Grummer beams: "I am so glad we share a love for the classics, Beatrice. Your grandfather, you know, was tone deaf and couldn't stand having the music programmes on."

I didn't know and I don't think I want to hear any more about Grandpa and his mean, bullying ways. When Grummer leaves, I turn off the radio and make myself a peanut butter sandwich.

Then I eat two more and call the doctor's rooms. The message on the answer phone tells me that the surgery is closed. However, in an emergency, I can call a cellphone number. I call it and the lady who answers says that the doctor will make house calls in the afternoon in extreme emergencies. I ask her if suspected appendicitis is an extreme emergency and she takes my medical aid details and gets my address.

I text Toffie and tell him to come round. I need some research material from him.

He texts me back: *Am wsanihg desihs and calenirg lsat nhgtis mses. CU ltear.* I gather he's washing dishes and clearing up the mess from last night. He'll see me later.

Two hours is later and Toffie's around. He says the skop finished at three o'clock in the morning when his mom booted out Tom and Candy, who had dropped in for one for the road after their game of Rummikub.

Toffie asks me if I'm very sick or if I can go swimming. I tell him I'm terminal and get my (Adore's) costume.

After I beat Toffie in three races of freestyle we discuss The Target.

Toffie says he doesn't know much about Dr Peter Waterford. He's new to the dorp and is previously from Bloemfontein, the city halfway between Jozi and Cape Town. I tell Toffie I know where Bloemfontein is. And it doesn't have any sea or wind — but it has lots of roses.

"But Ma says he's a bit of a dish. And he drives a beemer," Toffie says, peeling bits of skin off my back.

I'm thinking that the BMW driving Dr Peter Waterford's going to have to treat me for skin cancer soon and I put on some more sunscreen (factor 50+). I fill Toffie in on my strategy. After the house call and follow-up check-up, I'm going to take a turn for the worse. Three contact visits between the good doctor and Grummer should clinch it.

Toffie says this has to be it; otherwise we're down to Mr David Davis-Davis and the uglies. I think it's got to be it too. There's less than two weeks of the holiday to go.

When I get home Grummer's pacing. "Where *have* you been?" she asks and feels my forehead.

I tell her I've been swimming to try and work off some of the pain. And I groan and rush to the toilet and fake the kind of noises that Mom always makes the morning after the night before.

Grummer puts me to bed and then we wait for Dr Peter Waterford.

He roars up in his beemer and sweeps into my bedroom. I hide the hot cloth I've been holding on my forehead and make feeble whines and give him pathetic looks through my shades.

Dr Peter Waterford says I must call him Dr Pete and tries to give me a high five. I wipe his palm listlessly. He has a gentle and professional bedside manner. I make mental notes so I can add to my Target snapshot later. He asks me what I've eaten in the past three days and when I tell him he raises his eyebrows at Grummer.

"Seven peanut butter sandwiches and a double steak burger. Hmm," he says.

Grummer looks appalled and he looks appalled at Grummer. Good thing I didn't tell him about the ones I had for breakfast. When I was too ill to eat!

He feels my pulse, takes my temperature and measures my waist and wrists. He pokes my stomach and I groan even louder. But he says the pain's not on the appendix side.

I put a jinx on my biology teacher. Useless old bag.

"It isn't that time of the month, is it dear?" Grummer asks and I grimace and give her a negative.

"I can't imagine this child ever getting her period," Dr Pete says. "She is grossly undernourished and terribly thin." I think this child he's talking about is me.

He's mumbling to Grummer about chronic eating disorders and I'm not listening any more 'cos I'm counting the number of stripes on his tie and the number of hairs on the back of his right hand, and there are forty-two stripes on his tie and he has 145 hairs on his hand, which I think is respectable.

Grummer and Dr Pete leave my bedroom to go and talk confidentially about "family history".

They come back into the bedroom and Grummer's looking very weepy and worried. Dr Pete sits on my bed and tells me that I'm a very sick little girl and that I'm going on diet. It's a strict diet, which will be monitored for the rest of the holiday.

Tomorrow I'll be weighed at his surgery and

then a special diet will be designed which I will follow religiously. If I don't do this, I'll never grow and I'll be a very sick adult. I will have check-ups every four days. He asks me for my "buy-in".

"You can trust me, Beatrice," he says with sincere eyes. I tell him I trust him (not).

Grummer's standing by the door and she's mopping her face with loo roll. "Please, Beatrice. I need you to get better. Dr Pete's asking for a commitment to this process. We need your buy-in," she says.

I do a quick calculation. We're looking at four contact visits with Dr Pete in the next eleven days. I buy in just short of selling out.

I'm so bought in that when they leave I text my two and only friends back home with the bad news:

I win. U lose. I've pulled a doctor for Grummer. I'm a very sick little girl and u guys R going 2B even sicker when U eat that sheep's head. Send me the video of U eating Smiley by end of week. Your 1 and only friend, Beatrice Wellbeloved.

Chapter 18

GRUMMER'S KNITTING ME a blanket. She asks me what colours I want and I say black. Duh!

She sighs and starts knitting black squares. She says she will have made good progress by the end of the holiday, in two weeks' time. Correction: eleven days.

"Every stitch I knit I am praying for you to get better, Beatrice," she says.

Grummer's knitting in Dr Pete's surgery on Monday morning. I've been weighed and prodded and given my diet sheet. I've been set a weight-gain target of point five of a kilogram every four days.

Then me and Dr Pete "talk". He asks if I want Grummer to leave and I ask him if *he* wants Grummer to leave. He looks at Grummer, who's counting stitches, and he says she can stay. I say she can stay too.

Dr Pete says every time we see each other we're going to "talk" about "things". It'll help me get better. "You can trust me, Beatrice. You can tell me anything," he says with those sincere eyes. I tell him I trust him (not).

Our first talk about things is about Mom's many husbands. Correction: Husband Number Four. The one she pulled when I turned six. Dr Pete asks me to tell him what happened five years ago when Guido left. Guido? Who's Guido? My tummy feels like it's speaking in tongues. I start counting stitches. Grummer has cast on thirty stitches. No, twenty-nine, she's just dropped one.

I tell Grummer she's dropped a stitch and Dr Pete asks me again to tell him about the time Guido left.

So I tell him that Mom chucked Guido out of the house 'cos he was cheating on her. It's quite a funny story really, so I give him the low-down: Guido was a walker. He probably still is. Every morning he'd go out walking before work. He'd come back after an hour all red-faced and sweaty and take a shower. Then one day he didn't come back.

He didn't come back for four days and, when he did, he left again and missed my ninth birthday. And the reason he was gone so long was because he was trapped in the house down the road from ours and couldn't leave. (There was a power failure for four days in the western suburbs of Jozi and the security doors were all paralysed.) A lot of people were stuck in their homes at that time and a lot of restaurants had to throw out rotten food.

"And so that's how Mom bust him," I say. "It had been going on with the lady down the road for yonks and Mom never knew about his affair until the power failure. What a loser." And I laugh 'cos it's one of my top-ten funny stories.

Dr Pete doesn't laugh. He says he wants to know how it made me feel. I tell him it made me feel that people in Jozi needed to invest in manual overrides on their security gates. And that they should never keep too much stuff in the freezer.

Dr Pete says we can move on now. He wants me to tell him about Mom.

I tell him that Mom likes to drink vodka (Stolichnaya) and soda with a slice of lemon in the summer. And she likes whiskey (Jack Daniel's) on the rocks in winter. But when she has more than six whiskeys she doesn't bother with the ice any more. And when the booze runs out, she sends me down the road to the Dunkeld West Drankwinkel where she has an account with Mr Kay the bottlestore owner.

Dr Pete says we'll talk more about things next time. And I leave the two lovebirds to coo for a bit and I read the posters on the surgery wall.

There's this one poster that gives the average heights and weights for children. I'm one point fifty-eight metres tall and weigh thirty-nine kilograms. The poster tells me that I fall way out of the obese kid category.

When we leave, Dr Pete gives me a high five

and says we're making progress.

Grummer's very quiet on the way home. Two blocks before we reach the house she stops the car by the side of the road.

"Beatrice, look at me," she says. I peer at her through my shades and she reaches over and removes them. "That's better, now I can see your eyes," she says.

"Beatrice, why did you lie to Dr Pete?" she asks.

I look at the steering wheel and count thirty-two lines running all around the circumference and I look outside and I count seventeen figs on the fourth branch of a fig tree.

"Guido wasn't caught with the lady down the road when the power failed; it was your mother who left you alone in the house for four days while she partied with her fancy man. Guido was out of town and only got back later in the week. Don't you remember, Beatrice?"

I tell Grummer I've just remembered … I've just remembered that Toffie's waiting for me at the house 'cos we're going swimming.

Toffie wants to know all about Dr Pete. We're

lying by the jetty and I tell him that Dr Pete is a Colin Firth lookalike from the Nanny McPhee movie but with more grey hair. He's tall and built like a runner and he's got 145 hairs on his right hand.

Toffie offers me a peanut butter sandwich. I say I can't; I'm on a special diet regimen and can only eat six meals a day. And a protein supplement drink before I go to bed.

Toffie shrugs and the pig finishes off the sandwiches while I starve.

We finalise the strategy: I'll stick to the diet and see Dr Pete every four days. Then I'll talk about things to Dr Pete and I'll get Grummer to talk about things too, so that they'll get to know each other better.

Toffie raises a problem, the problem being that I can't get fat too quickly; otherwise the consultations will stop. I have a counter-problem: if I don't get fat fast enough, Dr Pete says he'll send me to a special hospital forty kilometers away in Somerset West. I tell Toffie I couldn't bear this. We'd have to start all over again and hospital doctors aren't as eligible as the ones in private practice. We need to FOCUS!

I tell Toffie I'll put on enough weight and when it looks like I'm heading for the obese kid category I'll do a bulimia thing to lose it all again. Toffie thinks it's a good plan. He says when the time comes he'll hold my hair back so I don't vomit all over it. I tell him he's just escaped retrenchment.

Chapter 19

I'M SITTING AT the dining-room table looking at the seven plates of food in front of me. There's rice, potatoes, beans, sweet potato, avocado pear, beetroot, and the last plate has a big steak.

This is called Lunch on the diet schedule. On the top of the diet sheet it says The Schedule!

I've already had two other meals called Breakfast and Mid-Morning Snack. And the two peanut butter sandwiches I sneaked after swimming with Toffie in the morning. Toffie says I mustn't tell Grummer. She'll freak if she knows I've been cheating The Schedule! I tell him I'm sorted. I did a mini-puke straight after, so she won't know.

Grummer's become the guardian of The Schedule! She arranges her "To Do" list around every eating slot: she has her walk in the morning and then we listen to classical music and eat Breakfast. She goes to Pastor Aitch for a prayer session with the bereaved support group. Then she has tea on the veranda and watches the birds, and I have Mid-Morning Snack. Then she knits some squares for my blanket. (She's already knitted twelve squares and has 128 to go.) Then we eat Lunch. Then she reads her novel and after Mid-Afternoon Snack she has a session with Mr du Plooy to discuss what he's done to the garden. Or she goes to the fund-raising meeting for the Die Trein crèche. Then she has her evening walk and we have Supper. She watches her soap and then gives me Evening Snack and the protein supplement drink.

We are on day three of The Schedule! Grummer sits opposite the dining-room table watching me eat Lunch. I look at the steak and shake my head.

I don't do flesh.

Grummer says I do now; otherwise she'll telephone Dr Pete. I tell her I don't do flesh and she heads for the phone. They chatter for a long time, and Grummer sighs a lot. She called him yesterday about the chicken and the day before about the fish.

Bingo! I must put him on speed dial.

Grummer comes back and says I can leave the steak. Dr Pete says we'll talk about "the meat issue" at my session tomorrow. I can't wait.

Mr du Plooy's loitering at the doorway, and Grummer invites him in. He sits down at the table, and Grummer feeds him my steak. He gets bits stuck in his teeth and I leave the table to go and floss. I can hear them talking.

"She's a very sick little girl," Grummer says to Mr du Plooy.

Mr du Plooy says all I need is a big klap on the bum.

Grummer says, "Oh no, Karel, not a smack."

And Karel, aka Mr du Plooy, says to Grummer, "What she needs, Mavis," — yes, he calls her

Mavis — "is a lot of klaps. You should give her one every morning with her breakfast. That'll soon get her head straight."

And Grummer says, "Derek (my late husband) and I always agreed we would never hit a child. I don't think Beatrice's mother ever had a smack in her life."

And Mr du Plooy says that maybe if Grummer had klapped Mom she wouldn't have turned out the way she has.

I come back into the room with squeaky teeth just as they're starting to shout and Mr du Plooy leaves soon after.

"That man is impossible," Grummer says and she reaches for her tissues.

I've made a list of all the things I like about Grummer. It's got three items on it and I add a fourth. The list goes like this:

1. Grummer has a routine. (I know exactly what she's doing every minute of the day so she can't ever catch me doing something I shouldn't be doing.)

2. Grummer doesn't drink (alcohol). (I never have to clean up her vomit.)
3. Grummer eats neat. (I don't get too grossed out sitting opposite her at the table.)
4. Grummer doesn't take attitude from hairy child abusers. (I don't have to get klapped with my breakfast.)

The list of twenty-nine things that I don't like about Grummer ends with "Grummer keeps on dropping her snotty tissues all over the house", which freaks me out.

I pick up a tissue off the floor and give it to Grummer. She says she wants to show me what Mr du Plooy's been doing with the garden. There are three men digging a bed on the side. They stand on their spades as they try to break through the hard ground.

Grummer says she took my advice about focusing on the people still living who would be affected by the changes she wanted to make to the garden.

"You're such a wise, wise girl," Grummer says and gives me a squeeze. I pull in my tummy, so she can't feel the peanut butter sandwiches.

"I hope your grandfather understands the compromises I've made," Grummer says. "But he's gone now and Mr September is still alive."

There's an orchard of trees at the bottom of the garden. Some of the more sickly quinces have been removed to make way for new quince trees.

"So, you see, Beatrice, Mr September still has his quince trees. And every time he sees a quince, he will be able to see and remember his late wife," Grummer says.

I look at the rotten fruit on the quince trees and hope Mrs September doesn't mind having bugs and bees crawling all over her.

Mr du Plooy's knocked down two of the shacks and left one of them standing, which he's going to convert into a gazebo.

"So Mr September can sit here sometimes and remember the days when they used to live here. Before they were forced to leave their home," Grummer says.

Mr du Plooy's laid out a vegetable garden and has set out a patch outside the kitchen for herbs.

"Your grandfather would be hopping mad if he saw the vegetable garden," Grummer says. "But you know, Beatrice, there's nothing like a home-grown lettuce."

I think Grandpa's very dead and not really up to hopping anywhere.

I look at the row of guava trees in front of the house and I ask Grummer when they're going to get the chop. And when the rose garden and pond are going to happen.

Grummer says she and Mr du Plooy still have to talk about all this, if he ever comes back. "But I'm going to have quite a lot of indigenous plants as well," she says. "Karel says the fynbos will attract the birds. And I do so love my birds."

I look across the lawn and see three hadedas pecking away between the weeds and I feel hungry. I tell Grummer it's time for Mid-Afternoon Snack. We must, must, must stick to The Schedule!

Chapter 20

I'M AWAKE EARLY today. I'm very excited. Today's my session with Dr Pete and we're going to talk about "the meat issue". Grummer must be excited too 'cos she's pottering around in the lounge and she's already had her walk. I go into the lounge and see her trying to settle a rooikrans tree in a pot.

"So, Beatrice, what is today?" Grummer asks. And I tell her it's the day we see Dr Pete to talk about "the meat issue".

And Grummer says, yes, but it's also the day before Christmas. And I say, of course it is and I help her decorate the tree.

After Breakfast, Grummer takes me to the surgery. Dr Pete gives me a high five and asks me to jump on the scale. And then he looks and rejiggles the weights and says he can't believe it.

And he tells Grummer to take a look and she says she can't understand it.

I figure from the expressions on their faces that I've made it into the obese kid category and I could kill myself for all the peanut butter sandwiches I've been eating. It's all over. I'm now a fat kid and won't be able to see Dr Pete any more.

Dr Pete sits me down and he asks me and Grummer if we've been following The Schedule! Grummer assures him and I tell him Abso-Lutely; I never lie. And Grummer narrows her eyes and gives me a skeef look 'cos she knows about Guido. Dr Pete asks me to take off my shades so we can talk "eye to eye".

"The problem, Beatrice," Dr Pete says, looking at me in the left eye, "is that you have lost half a kilogram. And this is not possible if you've been following the schedule."

He asks me what I think went wrong. "Come clean with me, Beatrice. You can trust me," he says. I tell Dr Pete that I trust him (not).

I notice that Dr Pete has seven brown dots on the blue part of his eye and I can count three hairs peeping out of his left nostril, which is a bit gross, and I think that when he and Grummer become an item like Brangelina known as Pevis or Mater he should ask her to pluck them out.

Dr Pete says if I don't come clean with him I'm going to be admitted to the special hospital in Somerset West (where I will be surrounded by loser doctors who don't have their own practices).

I consider the options, grit my teeth and tell Dr Pete that I've been cheating on The Schedule! And he nods as if he knew it all the time. He looks over at Grummer; she's stopped knitting and is giving me the crossest look I've ever seen. The line between her eyebrows is very pronounced and I hope Dr Pete doesn't notice her cross, ugly face 'cos he still looks like Colin Firth and she now looks like Nanny McPhee.

"It is not possible. I have monitored every meal

in the past four days," Grummer says and she purses her lips at Dr Pete.

I can't bear to see the lovers quarrel, so I tell Dr Pete about the peanut butter sandwiches. "But I puked them up," I quickly add. "Really, it was like I hadn't eaten them at all. It wasn't really a cheat."

Dr Pete first looks angry and then he laughs. He says it's fine and we're going to change The Schedule! so that I can eat peanut butter sandwiches in between my meals and my snacks. And I won't have to puke them up, because they will be on The Schedule!

He says we must now talk about "the meat issue".

"Tell me, Beatrice, why don't you eat meat?" Dr Pete's got a notebook and he's writing down everything I say.

I tell him it's a sad story and it goes like this: just after Guido left, Mom took me to a farm for the weekend. And the farmer, an old Mr MacDonald, took me around to see all the animals. And on this farm they had cows, sheep and chickens.

(E-I-E-I-O.)

I look over at Grummer and she's got her Nanny McPhee face on again and she catches my eye and I give her a wink. She snarls at me and attacks her bra strap.

I carry on: "And on this farm they were slaughtering animals. With a chop-chop here and a chop-chop there. Here a chop, there a chop, everywhere a chop-chop. And I saw it all and it was very, very, very disturbing. Very disturbing." (E-I-E-I-O.) And I put on my sad face and steal a look at Dr Pete through my shades to see if he's also disturbed by the story. He doesn't look very traumatised.

"Fascinating," he says and he reaches over and takes off my shades. He's looking at me like I've got a zit on the end of my nose.

Then he looks over at Grummer and asks her, "What time did you say Beatrice's mother was arriving?"

Grummer looks at me and says that her daughter will be arriving tomorrow morning for Christmas.

Her daughter. My mother. Mom's coming for Christmas ! I glare at Grummer. I glare at Dr Pete. I glare at the two lying, sneaky collaborators. Grummer rushes from the room.

Dr Pete tells me he just has to amend The Schedule! to replace the meat with vegetarian alternatives. There's a tap on the windowpane and I see a hadeda pecking at the glass. Dr Pete throws his pen at the window.

"Bugger off, vermin!" he shouts at the fat bird and closes the window tightly. He doesn't look a bit like Colin Firth any more. More like a monster from a horror movie. Then Dr Pete puts on his normal face again and gives me a high five and says that our talks are very illuminating and that we're making progress. He'll see me in four days' time and I must stick to The Schedule!

Grummer's hardly out of the driveway when she pulls the car over and rips off my shades. She's a little annoyed. Understatement.

"You stopped eating meat five years ago because it all went off in the freezer and you were stuck in the house for four days with no electricity and rotting meat and nothing to eat. You're a stupid, stupid liar, and I love you and you make me mad."

And Grummer goes for her bra strap, but she's left a trail of snotty tissues in Dr Pete's surgery, so she wipes her nose with the back of her hand. Eeeeuuuuw!

I tell Grummer she's got snot on the back of her hand and that she can't blame me for inheriting the liar gene. "You never told me *she* was coming for Christmas," I say. Oh, and by the way I don't love you and you make me bored. (But I don't say this bit; I just think it very hard.)

And Grummer tucks her hand away and says she never lied. She was going to tell me about Mom. She says she's sorry. I say I'm sorry too.

I'm sorry She's coming for Christmas.

Chapter 21

I'M LYING ON my bed when I get a text message on my cellphone: *Hwo did yuo konw?*

It's from Toffie. I text him back: *How did I know what?*

Aoubt DrPtee, Toffie responds.

I reply: *I knew 'cos he told me I could trust him three times. What you got?*

Toffie texts me back: *He si a klleir*. Which I work out means "He is a killer".

I tell him I'll meet him at the den in half an hour.

I get out my laptop and open the file on Dr Pete. The heading is "What Is Dr Pete's Dirty

Secret?" I've listed three possibilities. The first two offerings come from my two and only friends back home:

1. Dr Pete ripped out a young kid's liver instead of her tonsils and was struck off the medical register. Dr Pete is practising ILLEGALLY.

2. Dr Pete killed Mrs Davis-Davis three years ago while driving his beemer fast on the wrong side of the road. The driver of the tractor was blamed. Dr Pete is a RECKLESS DRIVER.

3. Dr Pete secretly fathered a child called Beatrice Wellbeloved fourteen years ago. Grummer cannot marry her granddaughter's father. It would be INCEST.

(The last one was mine.) I text them back and tell them they were the closest: *Dr Pete is a killer.* Way to go Dr "you can trust me" Pete!

I close my laptop and get ready to meet Toffie.

Grummer says I mustn't be long 'cos we have church in the early evening.

I find Toffie pacing outside the den. He tells me to sit down and he gets his notebook from the hiding place in the wall. He reads from it slowly, like a policeman reading a statement:

Surveillance Report on Dr Peter Waterford (aka Dr Pete)

Client: Ms Beatrice Wellbeloved (aka Boss).

Reporting Officer: Christoffel Appel (aka Toffie).

Okay, okay, get to it, Toffie. Give me the dirt. Toffie glares at me and says he needs to do this properly. He starts reading again:

On 22 December at 17:00 hours The Target is seated in a deckchair on his veranda. He gets up and chucks dogfood pellets on the lawn. When a flock of hadedas are engaged in their pursuit of food, he blows them away one by one with a gun. Surveillance ends at 18:30 hours.

I tell Toffie this is dynamite. He can continue.

On 23 December at 07:00 hours The Target emerges from the house in his dressing gown. He takes the seven dead hadedas from the killing field and arranges them on the veranda. Then The Target employs a biltong cutter (the ones for dried meat that look like baby guillotines) and chops off their beaks. He disposes of the body parts in the plastic garbage bags. Surveillance ends at 07:22 hours when The Target re-enters the house.

Toffie says there's more and reads me three more entries which expose yet further killing orgies.

I tell Toffie there's only one outcome from this scenario: Dr Pete cannot, must not, will not marry Grummer. There's just no ways she's going to buy in to his sick little hobby. Not with her being so cracked on her feathery little friends. It's a crying shame, but this is it. Goodbye Pevis. Goodbye Mater. And Dr Pete will have to see to his own hairy nostrils.

Toffie says there's also another outcome: "Beat, he's got to be stopped, man. It's a crime what he's doing. We must stop him."

I tell Toffie that he can't take things too personally. He needs to learn to leave his work behind him when he goes home. We need to FOCUS! I tell him to get Mr David Davis-Davis and the other uglies from the slush pile.

Toffie says he's quitting Project: Pulling for Grummer. And he's also quitting me. "You're sick like him, Beat. You've got no heart. I don't need your help. I'll stop him on my own." And he storms into the den.

For the next ten minutes he raves at me from behind the wall: just because hadedas are fat and ugly doesn't mean they're not special. They shouldn't have to die just because they're not endangered. "And one last thing, Beatrice Wellbeloved," he says, "they're scared of nothing. Nothing, do you hear me? When they cry, they have the power to wake the dead!"

Toffie's making weird snotty noises. I think he's lost it. I shout at him that he needs to turn in his gear and he chucks the cellphone over the wall. I catch it with my left hand. Yee-ha! Way to go, Beatrice Wellbeloved!

I meet Grummer at St Paul's. There's hardly any room to move. It seems like everyone from

Die Skema and Die Trein has checked in for the Christmas evening show. And to help themselves to all the goodies by the Christmas tree.

I spot Silas the closet albino monk in the pew on the left and he smiles at me. I wink back at him 'cos he still doesn't know *who I am*: the secret bloodline of Mary and Jesus. The living Holy Grail.

Pastor Aitch's sensational Christmas message is this: we are all God's children and He loves us all equally (even sick creeps like Dr Pete).

I look around the church and I see all God's children. And I think that Pastor Aitch's Christmas message would blow Dan Brown's petty little exposé out of the water. She should write the novel and get *The Da Vinci Code* thrown off the best-seller list.

We do a lot of singing and clapping and falling about on our knees and then Pastor Aitch says she wants us all to make peace with ourselves and each other as we go into Christmas.

Grummer and me hug each other awkwardly for too long and she murmurs how sorry she is about Mom and how much she loves me and I murmur back that I'm sorry about Mom coming for Christmas too and that she's standing on my toes.

Back home, Grummer tells me that I must hang my Christmas stocking by the fireplace and then we can listen to some classical music and I can drink my protein supplement drink.

I tell Grummer she must open her present from me. Now.

And she says, "Oh no, Beatrice, we always do it on Christmas morning."

And I say we always do it whenever Mom makes it out of rehab and it's usually the day before I go back to school.

Grummer relents and opens it and I can see from her face she loves it. She says, "What is it, dear?"

I tell her it's an iPod (MP3 player) with 3,765 classical music hits I downloaded, and I show her how to use it. And Grummer says she loves it, but she'll miss the adverts they always play in between the tunes.

Chapter 22

GRUMMER'S "TO DO" list goes out the window. We've just finished Breakfast and people start arriving to wish her a very merry Christmas. They wish me one too.

Pastor Aitch arrives with Mr September and they bring Grummer half a dozen jars of quince jam from last year's crop. Grummer takes Mr September to the bottom of the garden so he can see the quince trees and say happy Christmas to Mrs September.

Pastor Aitch and I wander around the garden. She tells me to look the length and breadth of the garden and I see the quince orchard and the vegetable garden and the blank space in the middle, which still hasn't got Grummer's pond and rose garden.

"It's just like it was forty years ago. Karel did it. He kept his promise." (She uses the word *belofte* for promise, but I get it.)

And then Pastor Aitch touches the guava tree with the markings *K and G Forever 1966* and tells me The Whole Story. Pastor Aitch tells the first half of the story in English and then when she gets excited she lapses into Afrikaans.

It's about a boy called Karel (aka Mr du Plooy) who loved a girl called Geraldine, who was the September daughter who lived in our garden. Then the troubles came and Geraldine left to go overseas and fight in the struggle against apartheid.

"And Karel promised her he would wait for her and she never came back," I say. This story is going on too long and the sun's hot. I don't have my sunscreen (factor 50⁺) on and I'm poaching in my own sweat. I can feel a swarm of freckles descending.

Pastor Aitch says, "You are half right, Beatrice." And I wonder which half of me is right.

She tells me: Karel waited and waited and Geraldine finally came back when the troubles were over. "She's done very well for herself," Pastor Aitch says. "Got herself a husband who's a bigwig in the new parliament."

Shame for you, Karel. What a loser!

"But look at the garden," Pastor Aitch says. "If she ever comes for a visit she will see it exactly as it was when she and Karel were young and in love. He promised her nothing would change."

I tell her I just have to get some sunscreen (factor 50⁺).

People don't stop arriving. Alan (with one el) and Greg arrive with presents for Grummer and me. Grummer gets a book called *Forbidden Love* and I get the full set of *The Chronicles of Narnia,* which I put with the *New Testament Stories* I got from Grummer (propping up my laptop).

Three bereaved-looking people from Grummer's singles prayer group arrive and I don't get their names 'cos I'm eating Mid-Morning Snack. One of them, a short guy with the saddest of all the three bereaved faces, gives Grummer a book called *Dealing with Loss*.

When he leaves, I look at what he's written on the front page. It says: *Dear Mavis, the hardest part of losing someone is letting go. Thank you for your prayers and support.* It's signed: *Your friend, David Davis-Davis.*

Then everyone leaves, and me and Grummer wait. And then we wait some more and while we're waiting Grummer extracts the soya and herb stuffing from the turkey. And then she rearranges the table again.

Grummer says we can't wait any more; otherwise I won't keep to The Schedule! So we decide to eat Christmas lunch without Mom.

"Where can she be? Her plane got in this morning. She should have been here hours ago," Grummer says.

I text my two and only friends back home and ask them for their offerings. They come back with:

1. *Georgia Wellbeloved has been involved in a*

fatal car accident with Mr David Davis-Davis at the turn-off to Hermanus. She is DEAD.

2. *Georgia Wellbeloved has met someone on the plane and has eloped with Husband Number Six. She is on HONEYMOON.*

I text them mine: *She's getting drunk in a bar.*

We finish lunch and She arrives. She's not alone. With her are her new best friends Tom and Candy. She met them when she stopped at the pubbingrill to get something to drink.

She says, "It's so bloody hot. I was so, so parched."

Grummer says, "Oh no, Georgia, I'm so, so surprised at you."

And I am so, so not surprised. I text my two and only friends back home: *I'm the winner!*

Tom and Candy have brought me and Grummer presents. Grummer gets a "lovely bottle of bubbly" and I get a milkmaid ornament with a crack on the nose which had probably been on the discount shelf at Tom's Anteekee Shoppee for the last thirteen years.

Then Tom says they might as well open the

bottle of bubbly and celebrate with Grummer. "Don't want you drinking alone now, do we?" he says (wink-wink).

Candy says they've been having the *most divine* time with Georgie (that's Mom). It was just *so lucky* they bumped into her at the pubbingrill. I don't think luck had anything to do with it.

Tom, Candy and Mom slaughter the bottle of bubbly over a packet of ciggies and then they leave for the pubbingrill to have "one for the road".

Before She weaves off, Grummer takes her aside and they exchange words. Many words like "For heavensakes, Moo, give me a break. It's Christmas," and "Yes, it is and you haven't seen her in more than three weeks. Please, Georgia, she's your daughter" — which I don't really listen to 'cos I'm having Mid-Afternoon Snack.

Grummer and me wash the dishes and Mr du Plooy arrives. He gives Grummer a book called *Indigenous Flora and Fauna of South Africa*. Grummer gives him a book called *The English Rose Garden*. They laugh and say "truce".

"Karel and I are going to look at my garden and

argue about the pond and the roses," Grummer says. And I give Mr du Plooy a skeef look 'cos I know that he thinks it's Geraldine September's garden and he'll never make Grummer her rose garden and pond. But he can't see my narrowed eyes through my shades, so he misses it.

I wonder what Toffie's doing and if he's found the presents I left for him in the secret hole in the wall. I've given him my spare cellphone and a book called *The Idiot's Guide to Texting* and I've sent him a message in Toffie-text which says: *Dear Toffie, Bewrae Rioo Dweuil. He wlli gte yuo noe yad.* (Which means in ordinary text "Beware Rooi Duiwel. He will get you one day.") *Your 1 and only friend, Beatrice Wellbeloved.*

Chapter 23

I SPEND BOXING Day morning scraping vomit off my bedroom carpet. I use the bottle opener I was going to give Her for Christmas to get at the bits of meat from the Prego roll she ate after her "one for the road" with Tom and Candy.

She appears at the door. "Aw, dolling. What can I say? There was something wrong with the Prego roll. I just couldn't keep it down," she says.

I keep scraping and she stumbles off.

When I'm done I lie in the hammock between the quince trees, and me and Mrs September watch the video I made with my cellphone when

She finally came home last night.

I've sent it to my two and only friends back home and they've come back with the following comments:

1. *Fantastic. Better than the movies. Put it on YouTube.*

2. *She's lost weight. Don't they feed them in rehab?*

The video goes like this:

Enter Georgia Wellbeloved. She spots Grummer sitting on the couch.

"Howzit, Moo. Where's the party?"

Grummer looks up from her knitting. "Sit down, Georgia. We have to talk."

"Talk, Moo, talk. I've got all night. What's your beef with me this time?" Georgia Wellbeloved heads for the chair and tries to sit down. She slides down onto the floor.

"Georgia, my love, things can't go on like this. They really can't. Beatrice is a very sick little girl. You've got to pull yourself together, so that you can look after her. She needs your love and care."

"Like you took care of me, hey, Moo? Like you

and Pop loved me? Like I don't think so, Moo."

Grummer gets up from the couch and sits down on the floor next to Georgia Wellbeloved. "Your father and I loved you very much. We showed you all the time that we loved you. We always wanted the best for you. I still do and I want the best for Beatrice."

Georgia Wellbeloved shifts away from Grummer. "Pop always wanted the best for Pop. It was never about being the best for me. Or you. It was what Pop wanted, and what Pop wanted he always got. Admit it, Moo. Go on and admit it. He was a selfish, uptight old bully."

Grummer shifts up closer to Georgia Wellbeloved. "He wanted for you what he could never have for himself. He thought he knew best what was good for you."

"But I was never good enough for him, was I, Moo? Everything I did was never good enough. Never, never, never good enough."

Grummer sighs. "You made choices that your father could not approve of, Georgia. But he still loved you, no matter what."

Georgia Wellbeloved laughs and she lights a cigarette. Grummer winces and Georgia Wellbeloved blows smoke in her face. "Ja, Moo. Like he loved me when Bea was born and he said he wouldn't have me home. And when Paul and Winston left and he said I'd made my bed I had to lie in it. He always loved me, hey, Moo? Like tell me, when exactly did he really love me?"

Grummer shifts away from Georgia Wellbeloved, who's lighting another cigarette from the stompie. "Georgia, my love. *You* left *us*. We were always there, loving you and waiting for you to come back."

Georgia Wellbeloved turns on Grummer and jabs her finger in the direction of her face over and over again. "Ja, and now Pop's gone. He wasn't there for you or me when he was alive and now he's dead. He's left you. Do you understand me, Moo? Pop's gone."

Grummer starts ferreting around in her bra strap and gives up. "Yes, Georgia, I do understand. I know he's gone. He's left us both. I miss him more than I can bear, and I know you can't bear it either."

Then Grummer gets up from the floor and says she's going to bed.

Georgia Wellbeloved smokes three more cigarettes and then the video clip ends 'cos she's wandering towards my bedroom and I had to stop filming from my spying spot at the door and jump into bed.

I text my two and only friends back home that the video was so totally yesterday.

My cellphone beeps and a message flashes on the screen. It says: *Roog Duiwel got both od us. She's had twims.*

I catch Toffie by the jetty. He shows me where Rooi Duiwel has her nest; there are two baby *duiwels* lying in the reeds. Toffie says that she's gone looking for food and we mustn't be near the nest when she comes back.

He says he has something else to show me and he takes out my (his) cellphone. He flips through some photos of Adore and him eating the fruit cake off a two-rand coin, and a couple of Mr Potato the plumber pulling Christmas crackers with Mrs Appel.

I say they're lovely (not) and Toffie says, "Ag, chillax man, Beat, I'm getting there."

He finally gets there and shows me three photos of Dr Pete's Christmas blood-fest. There's a close-up of the biltong cutter with bits of beak and feathers. (Eeeeuuuuw!) Then there's a close-up of a row of dead hadedas and two baby hadedas. (No, shame, Toffie man, show someone who cares.)

"Look at their wings, Beat. They're the colour of sun on petrol," he says.

I tell him I can't see colour through my shades.

Toffie says I must take off my shades.

I say I can't.

And then there's a shot in the distance of four black rubbish bags on the pavement. I tell Toffie at least Dr Pete's neat. If he didn't chop off the beaks the plastic would tear and there'd be rubbish all over the pavement. I give Dr Pete ten out of ten for neatness.

Toffie says he gives Dr Pete ten out of ten for evil.

"I'm stopping him tonight, Beat. I'm going there to get the gun and the bullets. He's going to be at the pubbingrill at half past seven tonight for the Boxing Day skop. Didn't your ouma tell you?"

Nope. Grummer's been a bit quiet today. The only time she said anything was when she offered Her some aspirin and told me to follow The Schedule!

"Your ouma's got a date with the killer tonight. While he's getting his jollies with your Grummer I'm going to be there by his house. And you can come too."

I tell Toffie I'll see. He says I must see what he got me for Christmas. And he goes and swims with Rooi Duiwel. I open the place in the wall and I see an envelope and inside is his precious Penny Black from his stamp collection stuck onto a card. I read:

FIVE REASONS WHY I THINK BEATRICE WELLBELOVED IS COOL

1. Beat is cool because she loves to drool (over peanut butter sandwiches)

2. Beat is cool because she rides her bike
   (like Lance Armstrong)
3. Beat is cool because she swims (with
   Rooi Duiwel)
4. Beat is cool because she has 33 freckles
   (10 more than me)
5. Beat is cool because she thinks (I'm cool)

Beat and Toffie Forever

From your third and only friend,
Christoffel Appel

Toffie's getting out of the water and he looks
at me and I say I'll check him later.
   Tonight.

Chapter 24

DR PETE PICKS Grummer up for the pubbingrill skop at 5:25 p.m. GMT. He asks me if I've been sticking to The Schedule! I tell him he can trust me.

He tells me I can trust him to take good care of Grummer at the party. I tell him of course I trust him (not).

Mom's having a nap on her bed after the little lunch outing she had with Tom and Candy in the afternoon. She grunts at me when I leave and I give her a grunt back, which means "later".

I grab my bike and meet Toffie in Dr Pete's

street. It borders the village green next to the Catholic Church. There's no sign of Silas the albino monk, so I know I'm safe.

There's a notice outside Dr Pete's house which says:

This is the private residence of Dr Peter Waterford. Consultation hours are between 9&5 Monday to Friday at the surgery in the Main Street. In case of an emergency, please telephone: 0824732726.

Toffie whistles at me and we park our bikes behind the church.

Toffie's strategy is as follows: we get (break) into Dr Pete's house and we find the killing gun and bullets and we take (steal) them and chuck them in the rubbish dump in the road by Die Skema.

Toffie says he's glad I'm seeing things his way. I'm doing the right thing. I tell Toffie if we can break Dr Pete's filthy habit he still has a chance with Grummer. I tell him I'm still FOCUSED!

It's easy getting into Dr Pete's house. The back door is unlocked and even if he'd locked it, all the windows are wide open. Finding the gun's more difficult. We look around the kitchen, but there's not a lot more going for it than high-fibre bran and rolled oats. I check in the freezer, but Toffie says only gangsters hide their guns in the freezer. Dr Pete's not a gangster, just a killer.

We search the lounge. Dr Pete's got a really lame collection of DVDs. He's got *House* (the first five seasons) and the full set of *Grey's Anatomy*. I tell Toffie I'll check out the study while he searches the bedrooms.

Dr Pete's computer's very interesting. There's a file on me called "Case Study: Beatrice Wellbeloved".

Dr Pete diagnoses me as being underweight with the potential for developing an eating disorder. He describes me as controlling, untrusting, unable to display vulnerability, obsessive, manipulative, uncommunicative, a consummate liar, having a poor body image, anxious ...

I see he hasn't got around to listing my bad

points.

He says some of my problems could be the result of when I was locked inside a dark house without parental supervision one winter five years ago for four whole days without electricity. Shame. Poor little Beatrice Wellbeloved.

Dr Pete's been a very busy man. He's written 7,456 words all about me for a medical journal. (I did a word count.) I delete the file and erase all reference to Beatrice Wellbeloved from his hard drive.

I'm just about to subscribe him to half a dozen rogue websites, which will flood his inbox with toxic spam for at least three years, when Toffie comes into the study and says he's found the bullets. They were in a jar next to the popcorn seeds in the kitchen. He's holding the gun. It was in an unlocked cupboard in his bedroom (along with some share certificates for a pharmaceutical company).

I tell Toffie to hang onto the bullets and I take the gun. I tell him we must go now before Dr Pete comes home.

Toffie says there's plenty of time; the skop ends at midnight.

But it's only 7:00 p.m. GMT and Dr Pete's standing behind Toffie.

He says, "What the hell are you kids doing here?"

Mom appears behind him and says, "Aw, dolling. What can I say? There was something wrong with the floor."

And Mr du Plooy's standing next to Her, and he's looking at me and the gun and he's saying, "Ag no, man, easy there, just take it easy there, my girl."

I'm pointing the gun at Her and Dr Pete says, "Give me that, you crazy freak." And he reaches for the gun. I pull away from him and the last thing I hear is the gun going off.

Boom-chakkalakka!

And the last thing I see before Dr Pete hits me on the side of my face with his right hand covered in 145 curly hairs is Toffie's face covered in blood.

And the last thing I feel is a chair smashing down next to me as Mr du Plooy takes out Dr Pete with a hairy left hook.

**

I wake up in the Hermanus Medi-Clinic six hours later and I can't say anything. My jaw's throbbing like a jackhammer and there's a tube in my nose.

Grummer's by my bed and she's talking to me all the time. When she's not talking, she's playing me classical music and when she turns it off she talks complete nonsense about Grandpa and her and me and Mom until she sees my eyes fluttering and then she talks to me like I'm a sort of sane person.

She tells me that she and Dr Pete were having a lovely time at the Boxing Day skop when Mom pitched up at the pubbingrill for one for the road. Then after Mom had taken more than one for the road she slipped and hit her head.

Mr du Plooy and Dr Pete took Mom to Dr Pete's house to fix her up when they found me and Toffie.

Toffie. I want to know about Toffie. Grummer says he's been moved from the operating theatre to intensive care and he's not receiving visitors. She says she just has to pop out to check on

Dr Pete, who's having his nose X-rayed. He's probably going to have to get a new nose thanks to Mr du Plooy.

I don't ask about Her, but Grummer tells me anyway. She's passed out in the next ward, but Grummer's sure she'll come and see me when she wakes up. I can't wait (not).

I ask about Mr du Plooy, and Grummer tells me he's sitting in the police station, waiting for Dr Pete to drop a charge of grievous bodily harm against him.

Later, Grummer and Dr Pete come into my room and he says that when I'm stable enough to be moved, I'm going to a special hospital in Johannesburg where I'll get my jaw fixed and can be treated for my "various problems". At least, I think that's what he said 'cos Dr Pete is speaking rather funny through his new nose, which looks like a wad of bandages.

I ask Dr Pete where he'll be going to be treated for his various problems. And Dr Pete laughs (I can see it hurt) and tells Grummer that I'm a fascinating little girl.

I want to know about Toffie, and Grummer says the bullet missed his eye, but there's still no news about any damage to his brain. I want to tell her that you can't damage what's not there — ha-ha — but my jaw hurts too much to talk.

That evening Mrs Appel pops in to see me. I pretend I'm asleep, but she sits by my bed and talks to me anyway. Like she knows I'm listening. She says that Toffie's being moved to a hospital in Cape Town where they have some big-shot brain doctors. She says all she can do is hope.

Before I go to sleep I ask the nurse who comes in to give me a painkiller and she says there's no news. And I ask the doctor, who's like twenty-five years old and I hope Grummer doesn't meet him 'cos he's such a loser, and he says there's no news. And the doctor says that while there's no news it's good news.

And when I'm transferred from the Hermanus Medi-Clinic three days later, everyone says that they're still waiting for news about Toffie.

Chapter 25

THE TRIP IS a lot shorter than the one I took with Grummer five months ago. We make it to the village in an hour and forty minutes. Everything's green and misty and the mountains are scarred with waterfalls.

Me and Mom get out the car and the first thing I notice is that I can see the mountain from the veranda. It's shrouded in a blanket of cloud.

All but one of the guava trees have been cut down. I check the fat trunk of the tree and I see someone's scratched out one of the initials and the date and carved a new initial in. It now reads

K and M Forever.

I look down the length of the garden and see a pond surrounded by beds of roses and beds of fynbos. There's a soft drizzle falling and the air is cold and sharp.

Grummer's inside sitting by the fire. She's knitting a jersey big enough for a bear.

I say, "Hey, Grummer."

And she says, "Oh, Beatrice."

And then she's holding me very tight and rocking me in her arms and she cries for a bit and then she laughs and laughs. "You special, special girl," she says, and she turns to someone in the kitchen and says, "Isn't she?"

And Mr du Plooy comes through from the kitchen, wiping his hands on a dish towel and he touches the itchy scar on the side of my jaw and says, "She's all right, Mavis. I told you all she needed was a big klap."

And Grummer says, "Oh, Karel."

And then Grummer says, "Now Beatrice, before you get any strange ideas about Karel and me ..."

"They're all true. Aren't they, Mavis?" says

Mr du Plooy.

And Grummer says, "Oh, Karel."

And I say, "Oh."

Grummer's full of news. She tells me and Mom all about the floods they've been having. The April rainfall was the highest it had been in forty years. Half of the posh houses by the river were washed away and the village was cut off from Hermanus for two weeks.

"Now they're trying to sell off the land by the river and no one wants to buy," Grummer says.

I say, "And it's going for *practically nothing*!"

Grummer laughs and says Tom and Candy have moved on to Hermanus and are probably helping to prop up a bar as we speak. Grummer glances nervously at Mom when she says the bar word, but Mom doesn't seem to mind.

She says to Grummer, "Everything's fine now, Moo."

And it has been fine for Mom and me. Since my stint in Johannesburg Hospital dealing with my various problems I'm as fat as a pig and my face is back to normal. Mom has been as dry as a piece of biltong and beats *Johannes die Doper*'s record by like three and a half months.

She told me that when she woke up in the Hermanus Medi-Clinic she realised that she had to make a choice between the three things she loved most in the world. She picked me over Jackie Daniel's and Stoli.

I told her I'd work on trusting her.

Grummer tells us that there's a new doctor in the village who arrived last week to replace Dr Pete (who ran back to Bloemfontein with his new nose and his gun).

I wink at Grummer and ask, "Is he as dishy as Dr Pete, hey Grummer?"

And Mr du Plooy growls, "Watchit, Mavis."

And Grummer says, "She's a lovely, lovely person. So young and full of energy."

Mom's very quiet while Grummer chatters on and on, and then Mr du Plooy asks Mom if she'll help him make the salad. I watch them through the kitchen hatch and I hear Mom telling Mr du Plooy that she's changed and that she'll try not to hurt Grummer or me any more. He looks like he wants to believe her.

When they come back into the lounge, Mom has puffy eyes, and Mr du Plooy says to Grummer, "*Alles is nou reg.*"

And Grummer agrees, "Of course everything is fine now."

I tell Mom I need to go somewhere and she nods and says I mustn't be late for lunch. I say maybe I'll go after lunch and Mom says I must go now. She touches me on my hand and says, "Go, Bea, everything will be fine."

The old bike knows where I want to go, but it still takes too long to get there. The roads are full of potholes, and the rain is starting to come down in buckets.

The green light on the robot is flashing and the pubbingrill's doing a roaring lunch trade. Through the window I see Silas wiping glasses while Mrs Appel chats to Adore. I get back on my bike and cycle on in the rain until I get there.

All that's left of the den is a pile of stones and rubble. The jetty's washed away and there's a mountain of reeds and broken trees on the bank of the river.

There's no sign of Rooi Duiwel and the two small *duiwels*. I look for their nest, but it's been washed away into the river and out to sea along with the seventeen posh houses.

I wait and I wait and the rain finally stops and I'm soaked through. I get my cellphone to check the message in the outbox. It says *Tffoie nad Btea Froveer*. I sent it yesterday.

I'm getting back on my bike when I hear him: "Hey, Beat. I got your message."

And Toffie's walking towards me, and I see that he's got thin. He's way outside the category for obese kids. There's a long scar on the side of his head by his left eye, and I tell him he looks like the baddie in *The Lion King*. And he says: "Ag, no Beat, man. Do I really? Hey, really? Do I look like Scar?"

I can see he's chuffed. And I tell him he really does.

And he says he likes my scar too. He says I look like Sunette the hairdresser after she came back from Cape Town with a chin tuck.

He says he's joking and I say I was joking too. He doesn't look like Scar, so there.

Toffie says he liked my message and I say I meant it: Toffie has Huge Pimples.

And he says, "Ag, no, Beat, man. That's not what it says. It says 'Toffie and Beat …'"

And I say to him, "It's fine now. I know what it says too."

Toffie says I must come and check out the new den he's building a bit further down the river. Rooi Duiwel and the twins have got a spot nearby where they're sleeping for a bit until it gets warm again.

I tell Toffie I have to go for lunch but I'll see him later.

He says he'll wait for me.

I tell him of course he will.

Thank you

I would like to thank Tina Betts, Megan Hall, Helga Schaberg and Jenny Hatton for helping to make this book happen; Hot Key for being so brilliant; and Mike, Emily, Sophie and Jack for everything else.

Glossary of Afrikaans and South African slang words

7de Laan – popular long-running multilingual South African soap opera

ag – oh

appelkoos – apricot

artappel – potato

babalaas – hungover

bakkie – pick-up truck

ballies – old men

biltong – dried meat, similar to jerky

blerrie – bloody (swear word)

boerewors – sausage (translates as 'farmer's sausage')

coloured – the ethnic label given to mixed-race South Africans under apartheid

dop – drink

dorp – village

drankwinkel – off licence

ek onthou – I remember

fynbos – indigenous shrubs found in the Western Cape of South Africa

gat op jou knieë – get on your knees

hadedas – large grey-brown African ibis with iridescent patches on the wings and a loud, harsh call

hierso – here

ja – yes

jis/jislaaik – wow

Johannes die Doper – John the Baptist

Jozi – Johannesburg

klap – hit/slap

kyk – look

leiwater – irrigation stream

lekker – good, enjoyable, great, nice, amazing

moffie – homosexual man

oom – uncle; also a term of respect towards an older man if not related

ouma - grandmother

perlemoen – abalone

ront – the South African currency is the rand, but some people (usually posh, elderly people) say ront

rooibos – redbush tea (a herbal brew made

from the South African rooibos shrub)

rooi duiwel – red devil

rooikrans – an acacia tree native to Australia and introduced to Africa

seun – son

sis – expression of disgust

skeef – narrow/skew

skop – party/dance

smiley – cooked sheep's head

spit braai – spit roast or barbecue

takkies – trainers or sports shoes

Transkei – homeland for Xhosa people, established by apartheid government

vrot – rotten

zizz – nap

Turn the page for an extract of *A Month With April-May* by Edyth Bulbring . . .

One

I knew Mrs Ho was bad news on my first day at Trinity College. I don't know her name when I first meet her, but I've met the type before: uptight, pushy, at school before the first bell has stopped ringing.

I'm in the corridor between classrooms – ten minutes into my first day at my new school and I'm lost. She's yelling at me. Loudly. Like I'm deaf.

'What do you call this?' She shakes my school bag in the air. My lunch box falls out into the passage, followed by my polony rolls.

I want to tell her that it's my school bag, but I'm on my hands and knees, trying to get the stuff off the floor and away from the sniggers of three boys who are looking at my polony rolls like I'm trying to smuggle hand grenades into the school.

'Blue.' She shakes my bag. 'Not red and purple.' She points at my multicoloured satchel in disgust. 'Navy blue. Those are the rules. Don't let me see this bag at school again.'

She tosses my bag down and is just about to stalk off when she sees my legs. From the expression on her face I think I've been amputated at the knees. Like paralympic runner Oscar Pistorius, except I don't have cool blades to help me bounce off to a gold medal and freedom.

'Stand up, girl.'

I stand up and her glare takes in my green-and-white striped socks.

'Do you think you're in the circus?'

I shake my head. Of course I don't think I'm in the circus. I'm at school.

'Take those off immediately.' She points at my socks.

She watches while I take off my shoes and socks and then put my shoes back on. I can walk around without socks all term until I get the regulation navy-blue ones. She says this and then leaves me sitting in the corridor, plotting how I can smother her to death with the polony that's fallen out of my rolls and on to the floor.

This teacher's trouble. I recognise the signs. I put her face at the top of my hit list.

I finally find my classroom and hobble inside, only to get allocated a desk at the back of the room with the class mouth-breather. Her name is Melanie and she goes out of her way to make me feel welcome. She breathes her boiled-egg breakfast all over me and whispers how pleased she is to have a desk-mate at last. She sat alone all last year. Why am I not surprised?

My seat with Melanie at the back of the class at Trinity College will be my home for my Grade Eight year. Home? This school's more like a prison. Blood-red walls tortured by ivy creep three floors up to a clock tower looming over a quad, its round face spying on the kids below, tick-tocking away the hours of our captivity.

Fluffy says if I mess up and don't perform to my potential he's giving me back to my mother.

Fluffy is my dad. It's just the two of us. There used to be three of us before Mom and Fluffy decided last year that they couldn't stand the sight of each other and split. They couldn't split me in half so Fluffy got to keep me. I'm not sure which of them thinks they got the better deal.

Melanie is the class monitor. She gives me some textbooks and stationery and says that all the books have to be covered in brown paper and plastic. These are the rules at Trinity College.

She also tells me that our classroom teacher is a man called Mr Goosen. But everyone calls him 'Finger'. I can see why when he comes into the room and takes roll-call for the day. As he calls out each name he looks up and then points, just to make sure that the voice and the face match the name on the clipboard. His index finger is missing in action so he points with his middle finger.

Finger comes to the end of the names and points his finger at Melanie. No, he's pulling the zap sign at me.

'April-May February.'

That's me.

My list of people who deserve to be poisoned with a side dish of salmonella is historically topped by Fluffy and Mom. Mr and Mrs February should have called it quits the day I was born, when they couldn't agree on what to call me. Fluffy thought April was the prettiest time of the year. Mom liked May. I got called a calendar.

Finger's middle finger wavers as he reads out my name for a second time. I stand up and stare that finger down. 'They call me Bella.' I nod encouragingly and hold nickies behind my back. I'm in the middle of reading *Twilight*, the first fang-bang novel by Stephenie Meyer, and I think Bella will do just fine. If I'd been a boy I would have gone for Edward.

Finger nods and lowers his finger. 'We have a new girl. Let's all clap hands and welcome April-May February to the school.'

He's obviously a slow learner.

After the class has given me a slow clap, Finger says he's got some urgent things to do and we must get on with whatever it is he's supposed to be teaching us. It's History. We must read the first two chapters from the textbook and then discuss what we have read among ourselves. Quietly.

Melanie tells me that Finger doubles up as the History teacher. He's also the Deputy Principal and has been around since the ark was built. He's hanging in at Trinity College until he turns a century, then he'll get his pension and go and open a B & B in Clarens – a village near Bethlehem in the Free State (as opposed to Bethlehem in the Middle East).

I spend the next two hours reading *Twilight* while the rest of the class text each other. I don't have a cellphone. I think I'm the only teenager in Jozi who isn't connected. Oh, and Melanie, who says her phone fell into the swimming pool yesterday. I tell her cellphones are last month's monomania of the mediocre. I'm waiting for my new BlueBerry. Melanie sounds interested. Her father has a BlackBerry.

BlueBerry, BlackBerry, what's the diffs? Melanie says she can't see the diffs at all. Then she paints her fingernails with Tipp-Ex and scratches it off with a safety pin. It's like dandruff all over my desk.

Finger comes back when the double lesson is almost over to check that no one's bunked off. He tells us to carry on reading from the textbook for homework and to think about History and things. I reckon he belongs to the first category of useless teachers. Finger can stay.

The next lesson is English. Call me a dork, or Boring Bella or whatever makes your cellphone whistle, but English is my favourite subject. The rest of the subjects can eat sand.

Melanie tells me that our English teacher is Miss Morape, who is sweet and loves Stephenie Meyer. Instantly I know Miss Morape is going to love me too. She is going to love me and leave me and *Twilight* in peace.

I begin rethinking our new best-friend status because the woman who walks into the classroom can't possibly be Miss Morape. She is not sweet. She can't love Stephenie. She's the one on top of my hit list. It is she who banned my multicoloured school satchel and has caused my feet to sweat blisters into my school shoes. 'Ho-ho-ho,' Melanie whispers.

I cover my nose with my hand and lean in to hear Melanie tell me that the woman in front of the classroom is Mrs Ho. She's standing in for Miss Morape, who's on a course to learn how to teach and won't be coming to school for the next two weeks. Miss Morape is definitely my kind of teacher. I miss her already.

Mrs Ho has the face of one of those babushka dolls. Her eyes are like tadpoles. They flash and gleam like a fanatic as she tells us to take out our Shakespeares – we're studying *Romeo and Juliet* this term. I think not. I carry on reading *Twilight*. I got it from the library yesterday and I can't put it down. I read until midnight last night, then Fluffy came in and said, 'Lights out, it's your first day at your new school tomorrow. If you don't get eight hours' sleep you won't be able to perform to your potential.'

I read for another hour in the bathroom, wrapped up in my duvet in the bath. The cold water faucet is faulty and water dripped on to my feet. I didn't notice. I didn't even notice when Fluffy banged on the door and said, 'Please, April. Please, stop hogging the bathroom. Stop reading that book. You're an addict.'

My name is April-May and I am addicted to Twilight.

Hello, April-May.

I tried to resist this book when it made the bestseller list, but I have succumbed like a billion other teenagers all over the world. I am an addict.

Welcome to Stephenie Meyers Anonymous, April-May.

I need help. I need to get my hands on New Moon *as soon as I'm done with* Twilight. *I need to feed my addiction.*

I read *Twilight* as the class reads *Romeo and Juliet*. Time passes and I do not notice Mrs Ho writing on the board. I do not hear her walking up and down between the desks as the schloeps write notes in their books and she reads Shakespeare.

Edward the vampire is leaning towards Bella and I'm just aching for that icy kiss. I lift my face as I sense his cold lips approach mine. I close my eyes. 'Kiss me, Edward,' I whisper. But when I open my eyes all I see is Mrs Ho.

Edyth Bulbring

Edyth Bulbring was born in Boksburg, South Africa and grew up in Port Elizabeth. She attended the University of Cape Town where she completed a BA whilst editing the university newspaper, *Varsity*. Having worked as a journalist for fifteen years, including time spent as the political correspondent at the *Sunday Times* of South Africa covering the first ever democratic elections, Edyth moved into writing full time. Edyth has published six books in South Africa and *I Heart Beat* is her third book to be published in the UK.